THE GREAT AMERICAN

THE GREAT AMERICAN

By:

MICHELE WALLACE CAMPANELLI

ARPress
ILLUMINATING IDEAS.
EMPOWERING VOICES

ARPress
45 Dan Road Suite 5
Canton MA 02021

Hotline: 1(888) 821-0229
Fax: 1(508) 545-7580

Ordering Information:
Quantity sales. Special discounts are available on quantity purchases by corporations, associations, and others. For details, contact the publisher at the address above.

Printed in the United States of America.

ISBN-13:   Softcover   979-8-89330-185-4
                   Hardcover   979-8-89330-187-8
                   eBook   979-8-89330-186-1

Library of Congress Control Number: 2024902448

DEDICATION

This book is dedicated to all those who are proud to be an American.

I would also like to thank God, my wonderful late husband Louis V. Campanelli III, my brother David & Greg and especially Fontaine Wallace, my personal editor and wonderful mother. To God be the glory!

A very special thank you goes to my friends and family members who have served our country.

Louis V. Campanelli III, JDC Officer Roger Campanelli, Navy James Pauline, Army Audley "Jim" Bullard, Air Force & Police Officer Louis V. Campanelli, Sr, Mary Louis V. Campanelli Jr, Army Steve Sigety, Police Officer Patrick Wallace, Firefighter Robert Wallace, Firefighter & Navy Richard Wallace, Army Rich Cook, Army Eric Popham, Air Force Amberly Snyder (Wallace), Navy Emmett Wallace, Navy Robert Jones, Marines Anthony E. Silva, Navy.

LORD, show us favor; we hope in you. Be our strength every morning, our salvation in times of distress.

(Isaiah 33:2)

Contents

CHAPTER 1

After the dawn of a new century in the month of September, Jennifer woke from her bed. The bright moonlight shone through her window, causing her to draw her lace curtains on the skyline of New York city. She glanced down at the long man sleeping beside her. His dark Italian skin glistened; his black hair curled in disarray over his stunning features. Suddenly his large nose scrunched up, and he snorted loudly.

Jennifer smiled; it had taken her so long to get used to that horrible noise at night, that deep snore that seemed more like a dragon breathing than her husband.

Slowly, she rose and slipped into her pink fleece robe, then stumbled toward the door. In her living room, she passed a hand-carved poker table with matching wooden chairs. On top was a pack of cards with a few empty beer bottles. In need of water, she ignored the messy table and padded to the kitchen to snatch a glass out of the cabinet.

"Jen," called out a man's voice.

She pivoted and discovered a man rising on his elbow on her long sofa. His disheveled blond hair hung to his shoulders. On his right shoulder was a large tattoo of a lion. "Charlie?"

He sat up, covering his short red boxers with an afghan. "What time is it?"

Jennifer glanced to her stove clock. "Four a.m. Who won tonight?"

"Not me, I got cleaned out."

She chuckled. "Wasn't your night."

"Karl won. I was up by a few hundred and bet it all on a full house but Karl managed a royal flush. It never fails. I don't know how he keeps winning."

"Karl's amazing." Jennifer agreed. "How'd Frank do?"

"Lost big time. And if that weren't enough, Jim told him he and his brother can't make it next month because of their sister's wedding down in Florida." Charlie rubbed his head. "Frank's worried about how he can replace them."

"Well, you know who I'll recommend," Jennifer countered as she opened up her fridge and poured water into her glass from a gallon jug.

"Frank wouldn't approve."

Jennifer shook her head. "I don't care what my husband says about my brother. David would never cheat."

"They play a lot of cards at the firehouse. He could have picked up a few tricks, Jen."

She rolled her eyes. "What about Vicky's new boyfriend across the street? Vicky told me he plays. Maybe he'd be a good replacement."

"I see his car parked outside her place at night." "Larry's his name, I believe."

Charlie scoffed. "Are you sure you want a police officer over here playing cards with Frank? He's already late paying that last ticket."

Jennifer laughed. "At least that one wasn't another for parking in the handicapped spot. Those cost us a fortune."

Charlie leaned back against the sofa. "I hope you don't mind my sleeping here. I just didn't feel like walking home."

"Still having problems?" Jennifer asked.

"Drank too much to haul my butt down the street, that's all."

Suddenly the bedroom door opened as her muscular husband stood in the doorway with only a pair of white briefs on. "Jen?"

"I'm here, Frank."

"Get me some aspirin, will you," he mumbled.

Opening a cabinet, she grabbed Tylenol from a shelf and walked over to him. Suddenly he leaned over and planted his full lips against hers. "You look sexy," he muttered.

"I'm wearing the same pink fleece robe we gave your grandma for Christmas."

Frank's dark brown eyes twinkled while he opened the bottle, drew it to his lips and gulped down a few.

"You have that meeting with Jack in the morning. You better not have a hangover."

"I only had two beers." Frank kissed her again on the lips. "Don't worry, I'll get back to bed in a second. I just want to clean up after these slobs."

As Jennifer walked toward her bedroom, she nodded towards the couch. "Good night, Charlie."

"Good night, Jen."

"I'll be right there," Frank promised, as she closed the bedroom door.

Jennifer removed her robe and collapsed back onto the bed. Instantly, she pictured her grandmother on top of their kitchen table, dropping the identical pink fleece robe and doing a strip tease. Then Charlie reached up and dropped a dollar bill in her giant panties.

"This has to be a dream," Jennifer murmured as she gathered up her blanket around her frame in her warm, cozy bed.

CHAPTER 2

Suddenly the alarm buzzed. Frank's eyes fluttered open. "Is it morning?" he mumbled.

Jennifer grumbled in response, "Time for us to get up."

Frank lowered his head back onto his pillow as he hit the snooze button, but it was only a moment before he'd started snoring again.

Jennifer rose from the covers and slipped on a black skirt and white polo style top. On the right side in small letters were the words "Sophie's Tea & Coffee." After she'd washed her face, she checked in the mirror. Her straight blonde hair was in disarray. Quickly, she brushed and pulled her locks into a ponytail using a scrunchie. Around her big blue eyes, she rubbed brown liner and brushed on some pale blue eye shadow. On her high cheekbones she patted on some rose colored blush. Then she addressed her full lips with fuchsia lipstick.

From off the dressing table she slipped on a gold bracelet, then grabbed a set of car keys. Turning to her husband, she announced, "I have to go, Frank, or I'll be late."

Frank rolled over and mumbled half-heartedly, "Have a good morning."

"You too, Honey, with your meeting." She hit the garage door opener button.

As the clanging door rose, Jennifer discovered a car parked in her driveway, a police car. She recognized the man behind the wheel. Passing the rose bush, she waltzed out. "Good morning, can I help you?"

An older gentleman in a dark blue police uniform got out of the car. He stood a foot taller than her, his short graying hair combed back behind the ear. "Hello, Jennifer."

"You're Vicky's boyfriend, right? Gary Hart."

"Hartman," he corrected. "Officer Gary Hartman."

Suddenly, across the street came a call. "Good morning, neighbor." A petite woman in a business suit sprang across her grass, dressed to the nines. She passed the Jaguar in her driveway and hurried toward them, crossing the street.

"Hi, Vicky. Good to see you," Jennifer greeted. "I was just saying hello to your boyfriend."

"I hope you don't mind but I sent Larry over to meet Frank."

"Frank's waking up now."

Just then the door to the garage popped open. Wearing only black shorts, Frank rolled a cart containing two rubber trash cans to the street. He stopped halfway, next to his wife.

Frank said to Gary, "Can I help you?"

"Gary Hartman." The officer held out his hand for Frank to shake.

"Frank." He shook the offered hand, then quickly released it. "Are we under arrest for anything?"

Gary chuckled. "No. I heard you have a friendly poker game here on Sunday nights."

"Nothing but a few neighbors, not a lot of money involved. That's not illegal, is it?"

"Would you mind my trying a hand or two? Vicky works the Jacobs account on Sundays, and I love poker. Back in Nevada, I'd play every week."

"How good are you?"

"I'm okay." Gary grinned, his arm encircling Vicky's back. "I hear your game is the best in the Northeast."

Frank nodded in tacit agreement with the exaggeration.

"Aren't Jim and his brother going away for a few weeks? Maybe Larry could sit in for one of them," Jennifer suggested.

Frank gave her a look; she wasn't sure if it meant shut up. "Be here at 8:00 Sunday, and it's BYOB. Drink a lot and you either crash here or walk home. We watch those things."

Gary ignored the comment. "You're a lawyer, right?"

"I practice Business Law out of upper Manhattan, Stan Michaels and Jack Peters PA."

"No criminal law?"

"I didn't enjoy representing people I knew were guilty."

"I don't blame you," Gary said and nodded. "You know my cousin works for Smith and Kacinski out of the Twin Towers. Robert Smith is leaving for Japan. James Kacinski is interviewing potential partners right now."

"I've heard of Kacinski. His office handles mostly mergers." Frank raised a brow. "Pretty prestigious firm."

"Well, I'll put in a good word for you if you ever want to leave your law firm."

"Thank you, but I have a meeting this morning to become a full partner. I've been waiting for this for a long time. But I sure appreciate the offer."

"Sure, no problem." Gary looked down at Vicky. "I better run. I'm on duty. It was nice meeting you all. See you Sunday."

"At eight," Frank reminded.

"Have a great day, Honey." Vicky gave Gary a pat on the butt as she paced towards her Jaguar.

Frank suddenly blurted out, "It will be a pleasure to take a cop's money for a change instead of the other way around."

Just before Gary bent to get into his police car, he responded, "That's right, a buddy of mine gave you a ticket for not wearing a seatbelt a while back."

"Thanks for reminding me." Frank chuckled. "I'll remember to pay it on Friday."

Jennifer and Frank watched them both leave. The moment the police car and the Jaguar turned the corner, Frank sighed and said, "He knows about that damn ticket."

Jennifer laughed. "Larry seemed nice enough."

"Lawyers and cops don't always mix, Jen. Why is Vicky dating him anyway? I thought she was only into millionaires who dine her in country club sand sail on yachts."

"I think she really cares about this guy. Be nice to him." Jennifer smiled. "He might wind up living across the street."

"Yeah, I'll be nice. Gary knows about my ticket, that I'm a lawyer. What else does he know about me?" he wondered out loud.

"That you've got a wonderful wife." Jennifer smiled as she kissed his cheek and walked to her car. "I'm going to be late. Bye!"

"Weren't you quitting Aunt Sophie's?" Frank mumbled as he rolled the garbage cans out to the street.

"Are you a full partner yet?"

"Then give her notice, Jenn. It's going to happen today." Frank placed the cart next to the road and paced back up the driveway. He had a troubled look across his face.

"You okay?" she asked, getting behind the wheel.

"A ticket writer at my table." He grimaced at the thought.

Jennifer knew he wouldn't have invited Larry to his game if it weren't for her. Sunday night was Frank's favorite evening. She hoped she hadn't ruined the game by bringing a virtual stranger in.

She backed her black VW Bug out of the driveway. Her husband gave her a quick wink just as she pulled away.

CHAPTER 3

Jennifer walked into Sophie's Tea & Coffee a few blocks from the World Trade Center in lower Manhattan. Joining the foot traffic, she slipped in between patrons entering the shop.

"You're late," proclaimed a woman's voice from the kitchen.

"Sorry, Auntie," Jennifer replied. She gazed over the black and white checkered floor and wondered if she would be next to mop it. Perhaps the large leather chairs and small wooden tables would require her cleaning services. The magazines and newspapers on the rack needed to be straightened, she noticed. The donuts and muffin supplies looked low. Maybe she'd be trapped in the kitchen all day for her tardiness.

"I told you what would happen if you were late again: extra duties." Just then a large woman with white hair tied in a bun rushed out of the kitchen carrying a pot of coffee.

"I want the coffee grinder spotless by 3:00."

That's worse than mopping and dusting! Jennifer stomped her foot and took the coffee pot from her. "I thought I was your favorite niece."

"Yes, you should see what I do to your cousin when she comes in late."

"Damn it!" Jennifer muttered under her breath.

"Wipe the outside good, too."

Jennifer approached the end of the counter where a man reading the New York Times had an empty cup.

"Need a refill." He lowered his paper as he requested.

Behind him sat a young man, mid-twenties with short sandy colored hair and big bulky muscles inside a blue shirt with FDNY Ladder Company symbol on his sleeves. Across his face spread an all-American dimpled smile; his blue eyes matched hers.

"What are you doing here?" Jennifer asked.

"Bugging you," he said, his eyes twinkling.

"Aren't there any fires you need to put out today?"

"Only hers," he said and motioned to Sophie, then raised his cup. "You really shouldn't come in late. You know how your boss is."

Ignoring the comment, Jennifer changed the subject. "My neighbor came over this morning with her new friend."

"Vicky's got a new boyfriend."

"You know—it's Gary?"

"Met Officer Hartman on a call. He seems very different from what I've seen Vicky with before."

"That's what Frank thinks, too." Jennifer pondered.

"Looks that way."

"Do you think Larry will be the man she marries after she dated all those rich engineer, doctor and computer programmer types?" Jennifer asked.

"I'm just glad she picked a man in blue. Not everyone is willing to put his life on the line for others. It's not a matter of money to a police officer, Jen. Becoming an officer is probably in his blood. Officers have a higher calling, to serve and protect the people of their city. In truth, it should be the police and firefighters making millions. Don't get me wrong, I never hated Vicky's other boyfriends, but at least Hartman has a reputation as being one of the good guys, a man worthy to wear a shield. What was that one guy who got rich off that scam? Alfred Van de…"

Jennifer laughed. "Actually, it was Kennedy. Senator Van de Camp was the one before him."

"A Senator? Figures. So, what are you doing later?"

"Cleaning the giant coffee grinder," Jennifer dutifully filled his cup and lowered her coffee pot, "for hours probably."

"I worked graveyard. I was thinking about catching a movie this afternoon."

"You and your movies!" Jennifer leaned against the counter and gave her brother a kiss on the cheek. "Friday, I'm off. We can go then if you want."

"What about Frank?" he asked.

"He's working late."

"How was his poker game?"

"You're still bitter?" Jennifer asked.

"I just can't believe he'd rather play with Charlie than me."

Jennifer placed her elbow on the counter and laid her head in a hand, gazing out the window at the businessmen with briefcases and laptop computers who filed past in droves. She took a long sigh and rolled her eyes. "Why do you guys care so much about a game?"

"Because, Jen, everyone knows that if you can beat Karl, you can beat anybody. Frank's been trying for years, and I did it. I beat them all and Frank's pissed about it."

"My husband thinks you cheated."

"I didn't."

Jennifer looked in his blue eyes. "You of all people wouldn't lie to me. Right?"

He stared back. "I won fair and square."

Suddenly another fireman opened the door. "Car fire, David. Let's go!"

David quickly donned his firefighter helmet and put his coat onto his six foot frame. "Have a good one, Sis."

"Stay safe."

"Talk to Frank about letting me in the game again. Huh?"

"I'll see what I can do."

Jennifer watched David bolt out the door and onto the long fire truck parked in the street while a siren began blaring. Soon the huge vehicle disappeared from the view of the large plated glass entrance.

"Your brother gets more handsome every day." Sophie leaned over Jennifer's shoulder and said, "My friend Fran has a daughter, a nice Jewish girl." Jennifer took a few steps towards a patron who was sitting in the corner, eating a Drewish.

Before she got around the counter, she mumbled over her shoulder, "Stay out of his personal life. Must I remind you of the time when David was in college?"

"How was I to know she had twenty-one cats and not his type?"

"David's taken now," Jennifer retorted. "And you know, so drop it."

CHAPTER 4

Behind the wheel of her VW Black "Bug", Jennifer spied her husband in front of their two-story colonial home, watering the yellow rose bush in their small yard.

As she drove closer, she admired her husband. Frank seemed more handsome than the day they wed years ago. She couldn't take her eyes off of the sleekness of his skin and the shininess of his curly, jet-black hair. He was like a gift from God, and he was hers, she realized.

She pulled her car into the driveway and jumped out. "Hi! Did you have a good day?"

"You could have called," Frank said. "I just got off the phone with your Aunt Sophie and she told me she kept you late cleaning the coffee grinder." Pointing to the dark stains on her pink blouse, he said, "You must have done a great job."

Jennifer raised her chin and gave him a quick kiss. "So how was your meeting?"

His smile faded and his eyes turned away. "Frank, what happened with Jack?"

Suddenly the neighbor's front door slammed open, interrupting them. A couple emerged from a large house to their right. A gray-haired woman was leading a toddler out, followed by a hunched over man with a three piece suit and dark ebony skin.

"Hello," greeted the beautiful dark woman.

"Mr. and Mrs. Cook, so where are you all off to tonight?" Jennifer asked.

"We're going to pick up Richie at the airport."

"Rich is on leave?" Jennifer asked, excitedly.

The toddler ran across the grass, raised his arms and gave Jennifer a hug. "My Daddy's coming," he shouted.

"That's wonderful, Gelsid!"

Frank patted the child on the head. "So how long will he be here?"

The older gentleman walked over with his golden cane with an eagle on top. "Rich just served his last day."

"Come on, you two," Mrs. Cook called. "We're late as it is."

Just then, a car rumbled noisily down the street. They all turned just as the taxi skidded to a stop in front of the house. Out popped a man in his late twenties, a suitcase in his hand. "Richie!"

Gelsid squirmed out of Jennifer's arms and ran down the driveway to greet his father.

"You've gotten so big!" Rich picked Gelsid up, hugged him and then jogged over to his parents. "I can't get over how much he's grown since August!"

"Getting more like his daddy every day." Mr. Cook grinned.

"Sorry we didn't meet you at the airport." His mother gave Rich a hug. "Your father fell asleep on the recliner."

"The plane was a half hour early," Rich announced. "Glad you had the taxi fare," Mr. Cook said.

Rich walked over to Frank and shook his hand. "Well, if it isn't the Italian Stallion."

"It's good to see you, Rich," Frank greeted.

"You still have your poker games on Sunday nights?"

"Sure do."

"Any openings?" he inquired.

"For an army vet, always," Frank said.

Mrs. Cook started heading back inside her house. "I'll get my purse and we'll all go out to dinner to celebrate. Would you like to join us, Jennifer, Frank?"

"Not tonight," Frank answered. "But we'll take a rain check."

Rich nodded okay. "So does Charlie still play?" Rich asked Frank.

"Never stops winning."

"We'll have to see about that," Rich said and chuckled. "What about Karl? Does he come?"

"Sure." Frank nodded.

"Karl still owns that dealership around the corner?"

"He got me a grand off my SUV last year."

"Not bad." Rich raised a brow. "Think he could make me a deal?"

"I don't see why not. You want me to give him a call and let him know you'll be coming down?"

"Sure," Rich said and nodded.

Jennifer gave Rich a big hug. "We've missed having you around here."

"I was going to stay active for a few more years, but now that Maria doesn't want to take care of Gelsid anymore… well, you know. It's not fair to my parents."

Jennifer agreed by nodding. "Your mom takes Gelsid to the park down the street all the time. You don't need to worry about Gelsid. He seems very happy."

"Oh, I know," Rich said.

"Karl usually works the lot on Tuesday mornings," Frank said.

"My mom has her hair appointment tomorrow. She'll need the car," Rich said. "What about in the afternoon? Will he be there then?"

"Why don't you just borrow my SUV? I took the day off from work. Jennifer doesn't go in until noon. If I need to go anywhere, I'll take my wife's Beetle." Frank fumbled in his pants pocket and pulled out some keys. "I'll leave it out of the garage tonight."

"Thanks." Rich and his father turned toward their seDrew with Gelsid while Mrs. Cook stepped out, holding a clutch purse. Jennifer watched the family reunion, then turned to discover Frank back watering the yellow rose bush again.

Suddenly she felt a rush of cold spray of water rising up her leg. Her hands immediately flew to her hips. "You didn't just do that!"

Frank dropped the hose and started to run towards the house, his laughter bellowing out. She ran after him, grabbing the nozzle to seek a wet retribution.

CHAPTER 5

Jennifer awoke to a screeching vehicle in front of their house. She checked the clock, 5:00 a.m. Noises continued: slamming of a door, the crashing of garbage cans in the street. Immediately, Jennifer nudged Frank. "Someone's outside."

Frank sat up, huffed and walked out into the living room; Jennifer followed, putting on her fleece robe as she walked. Finally, he opened the front door.

Half-falling out of their SUV, Rich parked on the grass sideways between their two houses. He then tumbled to the lawn, managing to rise onto an elbow. Then somehow, he sipped his beer with the other and began ranting and raving. "She should have known better than to marry her. Why did she have to go do that?"

"You took my SUV out for a late-night drive?" Frank interrupted.

"Didn't think you'd mind; I didn't want to wake you and the Misses," he sputtered.

"You drove drunk!" Jennifer gasped.

"I'm not." Rich tried to rise but reeled from side to side. Frank grabbed Rich before he toppled over again.

"Honey, make a pot of coffee."

Jennifer rushed into the kitchen, turned on the light, and then poured some water into her coffee machine and added a coffee pouch.

Hurrying back outside, she discovered Frank had Rich propped on their front porch swing as he reached to remove the beer can. Frank was demanding, "Give me back my keys."

Rich shoved his hand in his pocket and retrieved the keys. "I should have asked first," he mumbled.

"I didn't mind you borrowing my truck; I mind you're driving under the influence. I would have picked you up if you'd called."

"Frankie," Rich burst into tears but quickly wiped his eyes, "give me my beer back."

"Wait inside, okay?" Frank said to Jennifer.

She went in but sat down on the sofa just outside the window where the men were talking. She pulled away the curtain and cracked open the window. Frank shook his head, knowing that she was eavesdropping.

Rich sniffled. "Women suck."

"I was sorry to hear about your separation." Frank sat down next to him, raised his hand and softly knocked the window as a signal to his wife.

Jennifer lowered herself, then inched back up the moment she thought her husband was paying attention to Rich again.

"Maria couldn't take military life. She came back here to live with my parents. They were good to her, but she started having an affair, and they told me about it."

"Do you know where she went?" Frank raised a brow.

"She's living with the scum bag on Madison Avenue."

"Oh." Frank sighed.

"She visited Gelsid tonight. My parents say she comes three or four a times a week just to check on him."

Jennifer whispered through the window, "Why didn't she take Gelsid?" Frank grunted and repeated the question loud enough for Rich to hear.

"Why didn't she take Gelsid with her?"

"She couldn't bear to take him from my mother. They worked out this arrangement. Plus, I think, the scum bag doesn't want Gelsid around," he added soulfully.

"I'm sorry, Rich."

"She's so beautiful." He began crying again.

Frank asked, louder, "You talked to her tonight?"

"I met her later at the tavern."

"That explains it." Frank sighed. "Then you started drinking."

"Not too much, a beer or two."

"Or twenty," Jennifer mumbled.

"What?" Rich asked Frank.

Frank knocked on the window again. "Nothing."

Whispering, he announced, "Maria told me she's filing for divorce tomorrow."

From across the street, a large dark figure emerged from inside Vicky's house. He came down the street, passed his police car, and stared at the oddly parked SUV with the open door; he strolled up the driveway.

"Good morning, Frank," Larry said, tightening his long terry cloth robe.

"We didn't wake you, I hope."

"I think you woke the whole neighborhood," Larry commented.

Jennifer peered out the window. Down the block lights were coming on in a few houses while a few neighbors stared out their windows.

"Who the hell are you?" Rich grumbled with his head barely able to stay straight.

"Officer Gary Hartman. And you?"

"A friend of ours, our next-door neighbor, in fact," Frank answered for him. "He just got back in town from the army. This is Richard Cook."

"Nice to meet you, Rich." Gary glanced back to the strangely parked SUV. "So, were you driving?"

Rich raised his hand but missed Gary's extended one.

Frank held out his keys. "Rich had a few too many to drive."

"Were you putting some down yourself?"

"I was the designated driver." Frank smiled. "I haven't had a drink all day, unless you count coke and orange juice."

Gary nodded, then sat down on the banister; Jennifer realized he wasn't going to leave for a while. She quickly went to the pot of coffee now halfway done and poured two cups, placing them on a tray with sugar and a small glass pitcher of milk. She hurried back to the porch. "How are you, Gary?"

"Fine, and you, Jennifer?"

"Just great. Would you like some coffee?"

"No, but I'd say our friend Rich needs some java."

Jennifer handed Rich a steaming cup. "Want sugar?"

Rich took a sip and put it down on the porch. "This brother prefers black."

"So how long have you known Vicky?" Gary suddenly asked Jennifer.

"When Frank and I moved in three years ago, Vicky came and introduced herself," Jennifer said.

"Did she date a lot of wealthy men before me?"

Rich suddenly snorted, but his eyes had closed. Frank shook him and his dark gems flew open.

Jennifer shrugged. "What does that matter now? Vicky's with you."

"I bought her this." From out of his pocket Gary pulled out a black box and opened it. A small round cut diamond sat in the center of a plain gold band, shimmering in the dull morning light.

"Looks like the one that bitch used to wear!" Rich grumbled. "She didn't even have it on tonight."

"It's beautiful, Larry," Frank said. Larry looked at Jennifer's ring.

Jennifer knew her own diamond was twice the size. "Very nice."

"I'm afraid Vicky won't appreciate it."

Jennifer put down her tray and quietly perched next to Gary. "It doesn't matter the size of the ring; it only matters how big the heart is."

Gary smiled. "I'll keep that in mind." He rose and began walking down the two front steps. "I'll see you for Sunday's poker game. Oh, and Frank, pay that ticket, huh?"

"I'll pay it." Frank shook his head.

"'Bye." Rich waved. "Nice to meet you, Luke."

"It's Gary." Gary continued strolling away.

"We better get Rich inside before he wakes up the rest of the block," Jennifer said.

"I'll write the Cooks a note and put it on their door that Rich is spending the night at our house. That way when Mr. Cook wakes up to get his morning paper, he won't wonder why Rich isn't home yet." Frank stood and pulled Rich to his feet. "How do you like sleeping on a couch?"

He grumbled something unrecognizable.

Frank handed Jennifer the keys. "Put the SUV in the garage before anyone else sees it parked that way."

"Okay." Jennifer stood, smoothed down her robe, and walked to the oddly parked vehicle.

"Hey, honey," Frank said, pivoting with Rich. "That was really nice what you told Gary."

"I would have married you with something out of Cracker Jacks box," she admitted.

"Funny how you didn't mention that before I dropped a few grand on your ring," he said and shrugged. "I could have gotten you one of those lollipop rings, grape flavored."

"Gee, sorry I didn't mention it before." Jennifer looked over her shoulder and smiled back to the man she would have proudly married with only a cigar band for a ring.

CHAPTER 6

With the gentle rise of the sun, Jennifer tumbled from her bed, pulled on a pair of blue jeans and poked her head through a tee. She padded into the living room, passed Rich sleeping on the sofa, then walked out the front door to plop down on the porch swing. Her eyes focused on the two story house across the street. Now rocking, she waited for what seemed like forever.

From the house next door, Mr. Cook called out from a side window. "Jenny, is Rich still over?"

"Yes, Mr. Cook. He's okay."

Mr. Cook raised his right hand and pressed his black rimmed glasses farther back up his long nose. He nodded slightly, then tilted his head. "Tell him we'll go out for the newspaper later."

"Okay," Jennifer replied.

"Jenn, anything for breakfast?" She heard Frank calling from inside.

She headed to the door, cracked it open and whispered, "Shhhhh, Rich is still asleep. I'm waiting to see if Vicky said yes."

Jennifer scooted back on the swing, but she still couldn't see anything inside the Victorian style house she was eyeing. Slowly, she turned and checked out the whole neighborhood. In the far distance, the skyline of New York City unfolded, poking into the early morning gray-blue sky.

Across the street, Gary suddenly appeared in the doorway dressed in his police uniform; he headed toward his car. His large frame seemed to dominate the driveway. A man of size both in height and weight, he was a formidable presence. Few people crossed him, Jennifer surmised.

She stood up, hollering, "Good morning!"

Gary waved but quickly got behind the wheel, gazed over for a second at her and smiled. Magically, that tough face disappeared in that instant and transformed into a friendly expression. After facing the car forward, he drove off.

The door behind Jennifer swung wide and Frank asked, "Was that the officer?"

Just then, Vicky, in a two piece suit, flung open the door, carrying a large basket full of muffins. From her nails to her designer bag, Vicky was coordinated in pink. With her high heels clicking, she traipsed across the street and handed Frank the container of goodies. Fancy bagged coffee was positioned in the middle. "I just wanted to thank you; Gary told me what happened last night." Vicky suddenly raised her hand in front of her face and on her fourth finger on her left-hand sparkled Gary's ring.

"You said yes!" Jennifer jumped up, screamed, and hugged her. "That's wonderful. I'm so happy for you both!"

"Congratulations," Frank said and smiled.

"He finally asked me. I've been waiting for this since the very first day I met him. I'm telling you, I never believed in love at first sight until I saw him standing next to my car, asking me for my insurance and registration." Her face glowed. "I just couldn't take my eyes off of him. Really, I should have been upset because I didn't think I was speeding. It took him two weeks and four dates before he confessed that I hadn't even been three miles over the limit. He just wanted to talk to me; that's why he let me go with a warning."

"How sweet and slightly illegal of you." Jennifer giggled.

"I thought the coffee would help Rich. How is he doing this morning?"

"Sleeping off a hangover," Frank replied. "I'll get some mugs," he said as he turned toward the front door.

"Wait, Frank," Vicky said. "Gary was so nervous last night, he forgot to tell you. He spoke with his cousin at Smith and Miller PA firm."

Frank stopped dead. He riveted his attention on Jennifer and what she was about to say. He blinked a few times and then stuffed his hands into his pants.

"James Miller wants to interview you as a new partner Monday. Do you think you could make it?"

Frank pulled out a palm pilot from one pocket. Quickly, he poked his stylus to his calendar page. "September the 11th? I can postpone my first two appointments."

"Show up at 9:30 or earlier, floor 34. James wants to interview you before their office opens at 10."

"Are you going?" Jennifer questioned, disbelieving.

Vicky added matter-of-factly, "Apparently, James has heard of your husband's reputation. He's very interested in interviewing Frank now that Robert Smith is leaving to head their offices in Japan."

"You'd really leave Jack Michael's after just being promoted?" Jennifer asked, shocked.

"He gave the promotion to his nephew," Frank said and sighed quietly. "Tell Larry thanks. I'll call to confirm the appointment."

Jennifer's shock widened her blue eyes. She shifted slightly and touched his arm with a gentle hand. "Why didn't you tell me? I thought that was a done deal."

"I'd really make a name for myself if I replaced Robert Smith." Frank seemed to think aloud.

Vicky nodded in agreement.

"Thank you." Frank kissed Vicky on the cheek. "Congratulations, and don't forget to invite us to the wedding."

"I wouldn't dream of not inviting you two." She nodded, smiling.

Frank went inside, leaving Jennifer standing by Vicky. Vicky sat down on the porch swing next to Jennifer. For a few moments a pin could have dropped. Jennifer suddenly became aware of how different they were just by smelling Vicky's expensive perfume; it was Notoriety. Growing up near the projects before meeting Frank, she remembered working in a small clothing store for minimum wage and she recalled just how much that scent cost. She swore then she'd never wear it. To this day, even though she could afford it now, she didn't. Then a smile reflected between them which broke the ice. These two women from different worlds suddenly connected and Jennifer broke the silence.

"I'm so happy for you!"

"I have never been so thrilled in all my life," Vicky proudly announced. "I'm pleased about Frank, too." She grinned.

"Did you pull a few strings to get Frank that interview?"

"I make sure those who care about me get taken care of."

"What did you do?" Jennifer quizzed.

"Not much. They knew about your husband's work and reputation already."

Jennifer took Vicky's hand and studied the ring. It was a small diamond, maybe not even a half carat. In the morning light, however, it glistened. It was beautiful, a symbol of commitment by both. "I love it," Jennifer added. "You know, I have lots of rings. Some of them are worth more than what most people make in a year. But never," tears came in her eyes, "have I ever cherished a ring more than this one."

Jennifer leaned over and agreed. She thought about the meaning of the ring more than the actual appearance. Gary picked it out for Vicky and for that it had great significance. "It sure looks priceless to me."

CHAPTER 7

A Harley Davidson motorcycle revved down the street and skidded into Jennifer's driveway. Wearing a short brown leather bomber jacket, the rider parked and removed his black helmet. David's short blond hair popped out, crowning his handsome, boy-next-door features. After he placed the helmet onto the seat, he paced up the front steps toward Vicky and Jennifer sitting on the porch swing.

Jennifer's voice had a tremor as she wondered why he was here. He must have known Frank would be in.

"Hi." "Frank inside?" David asked, listening intently.

"Frank went inside to get plates for our muffins," Jennifer admitted. "You want some breakfast?"

"I doubt Frank will share a fluffy pastry with me," David responded, sarcastically.

Hearing the unusual tones, Vicky stood and brushed down her designer clothes to flatten the wrinkles. "Well, I can see you both have something to discuss. I'll bring over your wedding invitation in a few days then."

"Leaving so soon?" Jennifer said, trying to avoid letting her thoughts show.

"October 10th is our date. It's going to be a very small wedding, just a few of our closest friends and family. We figured our Pastor would come to the house and we'd have the reception in the backyard," Vicky announced happily.

"That sounds charming," Jennifer commented, obviously pleased. "Let me know if I can help with the arrangements."

"I'm not quite sure what to wear. Would you like to go shopping next week for a wedding dress or a white suit, maybe Saturday?"

With eyebrows arched halfway to her hairline in surprise, Jennifer replied, "I'd really love to."

"It's a date then." Vicky gracefully retreated down the front steps, beaming a contented smile. Jennifer returned the gesture. "Lunch is on me," she added. "Good to see you, David." Vicky waved back at him.

As Vicky walked across the street, David turned back to Jennifer. "So, is she marrying that police officer after all?" David gave an inward sigh. "I'd never put those two together."

"She loves him," Jennifer countered.

He cocked his head, watching Vicky enter her own house. "Good for her," he added, his tone calm, his protruding jaw unrelenting. "I know you always liked her. Guess now you'll have something in common: being married."

"You want to catch a movie today? I'm off until tonight." She spoke hopefully, not wanting to touch the subject of marriage with him. He had such a dim view because of his own situation.

"Okay," he muttered.

"We'll take my car though." Jennifer made sure he knew.

"Still won't ride my motorcycle, huh? You don't know what you're missing, Sis!"

Frank popped his head out the door. "Well, if it isn't the King of Fires," Frank snapped. "Or should I say liars?"

"What's it going to take to get you to realize I did not cheat? One of my cards fell, Frank. I leaned over and while I was picking it up, it dropped close to my sleeve," David explained.

There was a temporary, deceptive peace for a moment till Jennifer finally said, "If my brother says he didn't cheat, Frank, then he didn't."

"Get the hell off my property!" Frank said, abruptly.

"This is my house too, Frank, and he's my brother!" Jennifer clutched her small hands into fists. She hated this, despised it when they argued. It was rare, but when they did, it seemed to always be about her brother. She knew deep down Frank had never accepted David entirely and that even after years of marriage it hurt her deeply. Why was it a sore spot for them? She loved David with all her heart, and she couldn't imagine how anyone could not. So, what if they weren't alike. David was still her brother; his blood flowed through her veins too.

A loud horrible groan that lasted several seconds sounded from within the house, then a thud followed by feet plodding methodically toward the door.

Frank opened the door and Jennifer and David rushed in. Jennifer headed to the kitchen, grabbed a bottle of aspirin off the fridge, a glass of water and raced toward Rich, who was leaning against the doorframe.

"You drank too much last night," she reminded, handing him the medicine bottle and glass. "Sit back down."

"I feel horrible." Rich unclasped the bottle, took two aspirins, returned to sit then washed them down. "Can I have some coffee?"

"Sure." Jennifer went to the kitchen and began making a pot. She waited for it to fill a cup, then handed it to him with a noncommittal smile. "Here."

Rich sipped some java and laid back his head on a pillow, his hands covering his strong, ebony features. "How'd I get here?"

"You drove drunk!" Jennifer announced vehemently. "You should know better. You're lucky Gary across the street didn't put you in the slammer."

"I should be," Rich mumbled, wiping his forehead and then letting one arm drop to the floor. "I'm sorry, guys. Don't worry, it won't happen again. I don't think I'll ever see Maria again."

Frank looked back over his shoulder to Dave standing still behind him. "I thought I told you to leave."

His blue eyes gleamed inscrutably. "I'm taking my sister to a movie today."

"Not on that crotch rocket," Frank said, flatly.

Rich asked softly, "What's going on with you two?"

"What kind of person do I hate the most, Rich?" Frank asked, belligerently.

"Someone who disrespects your table." Rich slowly repeated the often-heard mantra, his expression turning to one of surprise. "No, not David?"

"Come on. We're leaving," Jennifer grabbed David's leather jacket by the sleeve and began tugging him out.

"I did not get my reputation as having the best game in New York by allowing cheaters in my home," Frank half-growled as he scowled at David.

"Let me prove I didn't cheat, Frank. Let me win again against Charlie and you."

Calmly and seemingly disinterested, Frank responded, mildly, "You couldn't beat me again if your life depended on it."

"I know I can," David countered.

"Well, how is it that you won so many rounds that night when you hadn't even won once before?"

"I'd been practicing at the fire station, Frank. We play a lot of cards between calls."

"You'd wear a short sleeve shirt and keep your hands on the table?" Frank questioned, then frowned.

"At all times," David promised.

"I'll think about it."

"I'll be waiting in the garage, Sis." David headed in that direction.

"I'll get my purse." Before she grabbed it off the chair, she heard David say, "You know, Frank, we're family now. You should have trusted me and stood up for me when everyone else didn't." And then he slammed the garage door.

Jennifer pivoted and walked past Frank. She didn't kiss him goodbye nor did either speak. She could feel his dark eyes on the back of her head and knew not to even look at him. Indeed, Frank was mad and when Frank gets upset, Jennifer knew, he liked everyone to join along with his unhappiness. Better to leave, at least until he had time to accept the evitable: he had lost a round to David.

CHAPTER 8

"I'm sorry for causing trouble between Frank and you," David apologized as he seated his large frame in the passenger's side of Jennifer's VW. He leaned his head back and shaded his blue eyes with a pair of dark sunglasses.

Jennifer moved her attention back to the traffic, then took a right at the stoplight. They moved past several apartment complexes before she responded, mildly, "If you ask me the whole thing is stupid. Frank lives for poker, but you should matter more to him than any game. You're his brother-in-law."

David reached into his pocket and grabbed a cigarette. He used the car lighter, waited for it to pop out, and then lit up. Rolling the window down halfway, he breathed out smoke. "I sure hope Frank will let me back on Sunday. Then I'll prove it to him."

"What? That you won a hand? I just don't get it," she said, matter-of- factly.

"Before that night, I had never won before. That's why Frank thinks I cheated. But I learned from the ladder company how to watch others at the table. That's when I began studying their behavior. I can read them now. Karl begins puffing more when he has a good hand. Charlie stops eating for a change, and Frank gulps down his beer when he grows more confident. I know how they act. That's why I was able to win so many hands. It had nothing to do with dropping one card."

"I don't know, and I don't care," she said with a pause. "To me, it's all a waste of time."

"Chess isn't a waste," David reminded, taking another long drag. "You used to play for hours when we were kids, remember? It's the same, but now we play for money to make it interesting. I can see where Frank's coming from. Since he thinks I cheated, he thinks I disrespected not only him, but also his friends. Since I'm his brother-in-law, it only makes it worse."

The car pulled in front of a large theater; Jennifer found a space not very far away. How lucky I am, she thought. For a while, they stared at the signs, reading about the movies now playing.

David finally pointed and said, "That one looks good. You in the mood for an action flick?"

Jennifer nodded, not really caring about the cinema feature. Her mind was on how nearly cruel Frank had been to her before they left. Why won't he believe in David's innocence?

After locking the car, David put out his cigarette, raced to get into line and purchased their tickets. Together they strolled inside. In front of the food counter, David ordered a large bucket of popcorn and a coke. Jennifer bought a chocolate covered English toffee bar and a water bottle. Back to movie 9 in the back theater, they sat down in the farthest row on the left, near the aisle.

How empty all the other seats were, Jennifer thought. "I guess it's kind of early for the matinee."

David checked his watch, knocking a few buttered kernels off his tub. "We've got about five minutes still."

"That's a big tub of popcorn," Jennifer commented.

A hand came around and patted Jennifer on the shoulder. She whirled around and saw a familiar face, with long blond hair, tight T-shirt, tattoo, and dark blue eyes. At mid-thirty, Charlie was handsome but weather- beaten, like a sailor.

"Charlie!" David greeted, raising a hand for him to shake. "How's it going?"

He took it and then pointed to the front. "I'm here with the Mrs."

Through the dim lights, Jennifer waved, although she couldn't quite make out the woman's features returning the friendly gesture. "You know I've never met her."

Charlie shrugged as if this wasn't the time, then sighed. "Well, I better get back before she eats all my nachos."

"Okay." Jennifer smiled, thinking how rude of him to quickly leave. She wondered if it was because David was here, too.

"See you Sunday," David said, very confidently, the older man, as he walked away.

Charlie suddenly stopped and faced him. "Sunday, David, you're playing at Frank's again?"

"Frank said he was considering it as long as I wear a short sleeve shirt and I agree to be searched before I sit down," David said, pursing his lips.

"Well, I hear an officer is coming this week too," Charlie said, coldly. "I guess he'll come in handy then."

Jennifer's face crinkled as she realized Charlie didn't like David much either, so she lightened up the tenseness by adding, "You'll like Gary. He's engaged now to Vicky across the street."

"No kidding." Charlie looked skeptical. "I think I've met him before on the ambulance. Tall, graying hair, with a slight beer gut, right?"

"That's Gary," Jennifer announced, shifting in her seat.

With the smile dropping off his face, David intensely questioned, "You believe I didn't cheat that night, right?"

Charlie lowered himself, moving in close to David's ear. "I know what I saw, Dave; that's all I got to say." He padded off to the front of the theater to sit down next to the woman who had previously waved.

The lights dimmed. An annoying, loud car commercial splashed onto the screen with a giant SUV screeching across a paved empty highway.

"No one believes me but you, Sis," David whispered, sadly.

"Does it really matter whether you did or didn't?" Jennifer wondered, unscrewing the cap off her bottled water and taking a sip.

"But you believe me?" he added, hopefully.

Jennifer laid her head on her brother's large shoulder and reached over to steal a handful of his buttered popcorn. Chewing, she admitted, "You don't have the heart to cheat."

David leaned his head down onto hers and with a big belly laugh announced, "Now you see why I get the extra-large tub. You always eat most of it."

CHAPTER 9

Staying up to see if her brother would be allowed in on the poker game, Jennifer secretly spied on players already seated around the hand-carved, ornate round table. Frank sat in the middle in the largest chair. Sitting to his right were Charlie, Rich, Gary, then an empty space.

Responding to the door knock, Jennifer quickly smiled at the friendly face awaiting her, that of her brother's. David had elected to wear a tank top instead of a sweater which was truly needed in the chilly weather. In his hand, he held a motorcycle helmet and his leather jacket. He returned the greeting, then lowered his jacket and helmet and entered cautiously. As he tilted his head, David's piercing blue eyes rose to Frank's and he questioned, "Well, am I in?"

Frank briefly shuffled the cards, smoking a long Cuban cigar, then slowly nodded yes. He looked disinterested, so David slowly approached the table, finally sitting in the only empty seat.

"I see you still haven't paid that ticket," Gary suddenly teased Frank, breaking the tension.

Frank deeply inhaled on his cigar and laughed. Smoke escaped his mouth in several large puffs. "I'm getting around to it." Then Frank began dealing out the cards, five to each man.

"Anybody need another beer before we start?" Rich asked, rising to go to the kitchen.

"I'm good," Charlie responded, his blond hair falling around his long, protruding nose. He checked his cards and lowered them with a grin.

After Rich grabbed a beer out of the fridge, he returned to his seat and turned his cards over. His ebony features registered no emotion, simply a blank stare, as if he weren't truly interested in the game.

"So did you find a car at Karl's lot the other day?" Charlie glanced over at Rich, gulping down half of his beer.

Rich discarded two cards on the table and signaled for two more with a wave of a finger. "I leased a Ford Mustang Convertible. It's a nice ride."

"Ten bucks." Frank tossed in a ten-dollar bill.

Every man at the table, checked out each other, then tossed in their money. Charlie asked for one card; Frank took three.

Jennifer watched from the sofa. She loved being around the men as they played every week. It wasn't that she enjoyed the game herself; it was the intensity that enveloped her. Charlie, Rich, Frank, Gary and David, incongruous by day, assumed combative roles at the table, testing which one was the cleverest strategist in the weekly game.

"I'll raise you a five." David placed five dollars in the center of the table, his inner implacability disguised.

"I'm out." Charlie tossed down his cards, his tanned skin suddenly looking weather-beaten, and he frowned from the stress of losing this round.

"What about you, Frank?" Dave asked with one hand brushing his very pale scruff surrounding his lips and chin.

"I'll see you," Frank said, astounded, tossing in the twenty and coming straight to the point.

"I'm in," Rich added as he rather nonchalantly placed his money to the pot.

"Me too." Gary tossed in his own green.

Dave folded out his cards, 3 fours and 2 Jacks. "A full house."

Gary tossed his cards down. "I've only got a pair."

Folding, Rich admitted, "I'm no good."

"Frank," David asked, so intently that a pin drop would have been heard in the silence following, "what do you have?"

Frank rolled his cards out across the table, one by one. "A royal flush." His arms suddenly reached across the table as he puffed on his cigar and pulled in all the pot.

"Damn!" David sighed with disappointment. Others groaned at seeing the stellar hand revealed.

Jennifer sighed, wishing her brother would have won. Turning, she flipped on the TV. The moment she did, a picture of President George W. Bush appeared on the screen on CNN. She immediately changed channels.

"Excuse my wife, she didn't vote for our new President," Frank announced. "She's a Democrat, just one thing I had to overlook before marrying her."

"Sore Loser." Rich chuckled. "Bush is awesome. How could you not like him, Jen?"

Jennifer stopped channel surfing when she came to a stand-up comedy getting laughs from a large audience. "This is about as funny," she responded.

David glanced back over his shoulder. "You've got to let the election go, Sis."

"More people in America voted for Gore. If it weren't for the electoral college votes, Gore would be President right now," she countered.

"Gore lost because Slick Willy got his penis caught in an intern," Charlie reminded, as Frank began to deal the cards for the next round.

"She has a nice bootie, that Monica." Rich gulped down more from his beer.

Gary snorted in disagreement, then looked over his cards. His eyes shot up for a moment to Frank, then returned to his hand. "Hillary's more his style. Slick Willy made a mistake with that young one."

"You don't think Hillary would be cold in the sack?" Rich chugged down the rest of his beer, then let out an enormous belch.

"The colder they are, the better they melt into your arms," Gary said, dismissing Rich's disapproval.

Jennifer spun around and shot them a nasty glance. "Is this what you guys talk about when I'm at work? And, excuse you, Rich! There's a lady present."

"Normally we talk about the weather." Frank finished dealing out the cards again, chuckling. "Aren't you tired, Honey?"

Gary changed the subject. "So, are you going to the job interview tomorrow Frank? I mentioned to Hartman's associate you were interested."

Taking a cigar out of the box next to Frank, Charlie quickly lit it and questioned surprisingly, "You're quitting Jack's firm?"

"I'm going to interview at Hartman & Smith PA.," Frank announced, leaning back with confidence.

"That law firm in the Twin Towers?" Charlie inquired, checking over his hand. His eyes suddenly focused downward, and then a hint of a smile inched across his face.

"One of my golfing buddies works for the firm," Gary informed, shuffling his cards around. "He said they're looking for an up-and-coming lawyer to become a partner."

With intensity the game continued; small talk mixed with flatulence and crude language. Jennifer didn't pay much attention after a while because her brother seemed trapped in a losing streak with no chance of redeeming himself. Nearing midnight, Jennifer could barely keep her eyes open, and the TV flickered on a late night horror movie.

Just then David muttered surprising words. "I'm in and I raise you all I have." He counted his money and tossed it into the pot in the center of the table. "$36."

Charlie folded, tossing down his hand on top of very little left over cash in front of his seat.

"I'm in." Frank put out his cigar. The smoke rose, partially obscuring his dark Italian features.

"Too rich for my blood." Rich placed his cards down in front of him.

Gary enriched the pot with his final $36. He had no more cash. "So, what do you have, David?"

David laid his cards out almost separately, one nine and then four remaining eights of spades. "Four of a kind."

Gary showed his hand. "All I've got is three twos."

"What do you have, Frank?" David asked, his eyes perking up with curiosity.

Frank let out a deep breath, rolling out his cards slowly across the table, two aces, two three of clubs and a seven spade. "Two pairs."

Jennifer sleepily watched David pull the giant pile of money in front of his seat as a smile stretched across his face. She jumped to her feet, elated. "You won!" Realizing who won had wakened her and she skipped a few steps to her brother's chair, then kissed him on the cheek.

"I'll be damned." Frank shifted back, his eyes gleaming inscrutably.

"You did it! I knew you could!" Jennifer cheered, enthusiastically. "All right, boys, what do you say we call it a night? Franks got an early interview."

"Same time, same place," Frank mumbled.

"I'll be here," Rich confirmed.

"Me, too." Gary grabbed his thick blue officer's coat from off the chair. He slipped it on and buttoned it, hiding his small pot belly. "I want to win some of my money back."

"How much did you lose," Jennifer questioned, wondering.

"At least two hundred," he sadly admitted; then he grinned. "But it was worth it."

Frank walked over to Jennifer and placed his arm around her shoulders. "You play great for your first time with us, Gary. I'm sure you'll do better next week."

Jennifer watched Charlie, Rich and Gary leave. Their shoulders were drooping but she knew they'd be back. They had just lost a battle but would never admit to losing the war. Frank escorted them to the door as she handed David back his jacket and helmet. He put his money in his wallet first, then grabbed what she held.

"Did you lose two hundred, too?" she asked her brother. "More like three," David replied. "But at least I won one round."

"You don't have to play next week if you don't want to," Jennifer said, worrying about how much he'd lost. She knew about his bills. He didn't make that much as a firefighter.

Together, they approached the door. As he passed Frank, David announced, "See you next Sunday, brother."

Dave kissed his sister on his cheek and headed out the door. "Oh, and Frank, an apology might be nice, now that you know I can win on my own."

Frank rolled his hazel eyes but gave David a quick pat on the back. "Don't press your luck, Fire King. That only proves you didn't cheat tonight."

David skipped down the steps, slipping on his jacket. It was a cold night; his breath formed white puffs as he wished them a good night.

Suddenly Frank slammed the door and swept Jennifer into a big, deep, long kiss. She melted in his arms. Feeling him so passionate made her tremble in response.

"I take it you won a lot."

"Oh yeah," he said and grinned.

"Thanks for letting my brother play again."

"You know, I might have been wrong about him," Frank said, winking. "But I don't think so and right now, I don't care."

CHAPTER 10

The next morning, Jennifer was finishing her bagel as Frank stumbled out of the bedroom. Dressed to the nines in a pin-striped business suit, he buttoned his white shirt.

Jennifer rose and greeted him with a good morning kiss. In her best imitation of Billy Crystal she said, "You look ma-ah-velous!"

He pulled at his silk tie, which hung slightly to the right. "I called Jack and told him to postpone my appointments because I wasn't feeling well. I'm taking a paid sick day."

"I'm sorry you had to lie."

"Me too," he said amicably, glancing into the mirror. He fiddled a moment longer with his tie and then faced her. "I'll drop you off around 8:30, leave the car, walk a few blocks to the interview, then catch a cab."

"Are you sure you want to drive me?" she questioned, pleasantly.

"I don't want to deal with finding a parking space today." Frank checked his reflection one last time and ran a hand through his thick black hair. "I'll meet you at home. You work only the morning shift, right?"

"Are you nervous?" She smiled back, knowing he was.

He took a deep breath. "If I get this job, it will change everything. We could move into a bigger house…and you can finally quit Aunt Sophie's."

"I love our house," Jennifer admitted, appreciatively; then she rubbed her belly. "I don't want a larger house, maybe just a bigger family."

"Oh no, here it comes, the baby talk." He shook his head and raised his prominent chin. "I've got to make more money first before we should try."

Jennifer straightened his tie which still listed to the right. Deciding that this wasn't the time to inform him that she might already be pregnant, she encouraged him instead. "You'll do great, Honey. Just be yourself and everyone will respond positively to you."

Frank wrapped his arm around her and kissed her on the forehead. "Thanks. You ready?"

She nodded yes and they ambled to the garage door where Frank punched the door opener. After getting in the VW, Frank backed out of the driveway. In the connecting side yard, Gelsid was holding up his mitt as Rich mimed a quick underhand toss.

Frank greeted Rich with a quick nod. "Good morning."

Rich waved back. "Good luck at the interview!"

As the VW bug puttered down the road, neither one spoke, but they held hands next to the gear shaft. Jennifer's head leaned back and watched the city skyline of New York City growing closer. What a calming ride, she decided. It didn't seem long until Frank reached the back of the Java & Breakfast shop and parked. After he passed around the car, he opened the door for her.

Grabbing her purse, she checked her simple tan leather-banded watch. "It's only 8:25. You'll be early."

"Better to appear eager."

Inside the front door of the coffee shop, Jennifer looked over the store full of customers who grasped coffee cups and read newspapers while they sat around small tables. Frank waved to Aunt Sophie behind the counter, then opened the door.

"I'll see you later," he muttered quickly to Jennifer.

"Call me so I'll know how it went!" she replied, suddenly worried about his nerves. She remembered when Frank went to an interview years before, he forgot to bring a pen and the employer sent him home without even speaking to him further.

"You have a pen, right?"

Frank stuffed his hand in his inner jacket pocket and huffed. "Yes, but I forgot the cell."

"Use a pay phone in the lobby."

"What is your handsome husband dressed up for? Does he have court this morning?" Aunt Sophie shuffled closer, refilling a customer's mug of coffee. She glanced up through small, round spectacles.

"Should I tell her?" Frank whispered.

Jennifer burst out, proudly, "Frank has an interview this morning at a law firm in the twin towers."

"Good for you, honey!" Then she padded over to the next patron who was holding up his coffee mug.

Frank shut the door and hustled out to the street. For a moment Jennifer watched her handsome, nervous husband. His normal Italian swagger was faster, and he kept threading his fingers through his dark curls, his nervous habit.

"This coffee isn't going to pour itself." The raised voice of her Aunt tore Jennifer away from her reverie. Jennifer moved away from the glass store front; she tied on her apron and hurried around the back of the long white counter.

"You want the radio on?" Jennifer asked, nearing the cappuccino machine.

"Sure, we're low on omelet peppers. Get right on to chopping."

Jennifer pivoted, flipped on the radio to a light rock station, and slipped through the kitchen doors. From the right of the stove, she snatched a bag of green peppers and began to cut several open, dug out the seeds, hurried to the sink, and rinsed out the hulls. Forcing the peppers flat, she began dicing, one vegetable at a time. Aunt Sophie swung through the kitchen door, poking her head in. "I'm going to need you to go to the store and pick up some onions next."

"I'll…" Jennifer stopped mid-sentence as an ear-splitting rattle shook the windows.

"Must have been a car crash." Aunt Sophie rushed out to check.

A few minutes passed, then Jennifer heard ambulances and fire truck sirens whizzing past the shop. She put down her knife and went out the kitchen door to see for herself. Aunt Sophie and every patron were now standing near the glass, peering oddly up.

Aunt Sophie rushed over to her. "Which tower was Frank going to?"

"Why?" she asked, aghast.

"A plane just crashed into one—the radio just announced it," she announced in one breath.

"You're kidding?" Jennifer's eyebrows jumped halfway to her hairline in shock.

"No-o-o." Aunt Sophie's face turned ashen. She grabbed Jennifer's arm and began leading her to the window. Outside no one was moving down the street; they just stared up, hypnotized and in horror of what they'd just witnessed.

With heart pumping, Jennifer glanced near the top of the tower where smoke and flames exuded from a giant gaping hole. "Oh, no!"

"Frank might not be in that tower," Aunt Sophie quickly interjected. "Which one was he going to?"

"I don't know! I didn't even ask! They'd evacuate both, wouldn't they?" Jennifer suddenly felt faint. Her mind immediately pictured the worst: Frank was there on the floor where the airplane hit. She began to shake. She couldn't believe that this could happen. How could it? Wasn't the pilot trained? Didn't he see the building? How could anyone just run an airplane into a giant skyscraper! Something must have been wrong, right? The plane became uncontrollable perhaps? It just swerved? What happened just seconds before? My God, how could this occur at all? And Frank might have been on that floor!

"We'll look in the phone book," Aunt Sophie nervously said. "Do you remember the company's name where he was going for the interview?"

"Don't bother. I'm going down there." Jennifer took off her apron. "I have to make sure he's okay myself."

Sirens screeched from another passing ambulance.

"No, it's too dangerous." Aunt Sophie pulled Jennifer behind the counter. She pulled out a phone and plopped it down. "Where was he going?"

"Hartman and Smith! I think it's those names."

Aunt Sophie began turning through the yellow pages. "What would lawyers be under?" Suddenly screams resonated from outside.

Jennifer ran out, just in time to see a second jet plane crashing into the center of the other tower. Bam! Another bone chilling tremor rocked the second building.

Crying out her husband's name, Jennifer felt Aunt Sophie's arms about her. "Frank!"

Everyone around them began to scatter to their cars, to their offices, to safer destinations. Jennifer could barely breathe; her heart jackhammered. Without contemplation, she pulled out of Aunt Sophie's grasp and tore off down the street toward the two massive towers, both now billowing smoke.

CHAPTER 11

As Jennifer ran, she wondered if Frank could be trapped in an elevator or in the stairwell; she cut to the left. Bystanders stood mesmerized by the sight of the two giant, towering infernos. The second plane crashed lower, Jennifer realized. For the life of her, she couldn't remember what floor Smith P.A. was on. Had Frank mentioned a number? Wasn't there another lawyer's name?

Suddenly arms grabbed her from behind. "Sis, it's me!"

Jennifer looked up to discover her brother David outfitted in firefighting gear. Before her in the middle of the street, his fire truck sat surrounded by honking traffic.

"Frank's in a tower!" she gasped.

"Get back to Aunt Sophie's. It's too dangerous out here. I'll get Frank! I'll make sure he gets home," he ordered.

Hearing a roar like a freight train, Jennifer looked up in horror. Above her, the first tower began to crumble. Then she felt nothing beneath her feet; her brother had swept her up and was carrying her off.

Glancing over his shoulder, she saw the building tumbling downward; an enormous cloud of dust billowed out like a twirling giant skirt as bystanders scattered in different directions. An acrid smell permeated the air. For a brief moment, she wondered if all this was real or a terrifying nightmare. Was this a horror movie? Were people truly running for their lives?

As the building tumbled, a thick smoke enveloped her; she gasped for breath. She could hardly see a foot in front of her face. It was as if day had become night.

Suddenly, a mask was thrown in front of her mouth, and she heard, "Take two breaths and hold it!"

She did and in a brief moment she could no longer open her eyes; they stung as if splinters had invaded. Then the mask was removed and brought to her brother's ash-covered face. Quickly he returned the mask to her and then repeated this process. His hand pushed open a glass door and she realized he had carried her back inside Aunt Sophie's. Many patrons inside were also covered in white soot from head to toe.

"Shut the door!" one yelled.

Aunt Sophie's arms encircled them both. "Are you two all right?"

"The first building collapsed," David said and coughed. "I never thought it would."

"I couldn't find Frank!" Jennifer shouted.

"Sis, which building was he in?" David whirled her around.

She could barely see his face through her narrowed, teary slits. "He went there for an interview at Smith P.A. I don't know what floor! Why didn't I ask him? Oh why?" she wailed.

David returned the mask to cover his face.

Aunt Sophie grabbed him. "You are not going back out there!"

David suddenly grabbed a marker out of his jacket and scribbled his name and a number on his arm. He pulled down his coat sleeve. "Sis, get in your car and drive home. I'm going to find Frank and make sure he goes straight there. If he's hurt, I'll get him to the hospital and call you. Do you understand me? Wait there."

Jennifer wiped her eyes. "Yes."

"Repeat what I said."

"I'm to get in my car…" she gasped, "and drive home. You'll find Frank and bring him to me."

"That's right." He hugged her, tightly.

Suddenly, she realized why he wrote numbers on his arm: if he were lying somewhere, the rescuers would know his identity. Her brother was going into the other building that very well might tumble just like the first.

She tried to grab him, but his slick coat slipped from her fingers. "Dave, wait!"

The door burst open, and he flew out. "I love you!" he shouted back. Even over the noise of sirens and people screaming, she heard those words.

Aunt Sophie started wiping her cheeks with a wet cloth. "I'll drive you home," she said.

"You can't kick us out!" a customer retorted.

"What about us? You can't force us back out there. We won't be able to breathe," another added.

Jennifer realized her aunt couldn't lock everyone out nor leave. "I'll drive myself. Dave, Frank, everyone is okay. Frank was on a lower floor, I'm sure. He must have gotten out. I'll do what Dave wants. Who knows; he might have already found him and is getting him to safety."

Gently, Aunt Sophie kissed her cheek.

Jennifer grabbed her purse and raced to the door, shutting it quickly so as to not let in more smoke. She held her breath, closed her eyes as much as she could and rushed to her car, now covered in gray soot. She jumped inside and took a deep breath; her car's air smelled clean. She started the engine, shut off the air conditioning and started down the crowded road.

Quickly she turned on her wipers, which only streaked the windshield, leaving barely enough space for her to see. Slowly, she backed out of her space when another horrifying noise thundered, a sound she now recognized.

She couldn't look; she didn't want to look. It couldn't be!

Like the Devil reaching out, smoke enveloped her car. She sped as much as traffic permitted, trying to outrun the scattering debris. She finally managed to beat the smoke belching out of lower Manhattan. Her eyes filled with tears and her chest hurt as she pulled over to the curb and shut off the engine. Across the water she could see the island palled in smoke as if a nuclear bomb had exploded; the entire city was blanketed. In her side mirror, she now realized that the second building had completely disappeared. She took a breath. "God, please…I beg you. Let Frank and Dave be all right. Please, God!"

With a flick of the key, she restarted her car, drove several miles and finally pulled into her own street. Vicky stood outside, staring at the skyline of the city, now nearly obscured by smoky ash.

Running to Jen's VW as it pulled into her home driveway, Vicky shouted, "Jennifer, what happened? Jennifer?"

A thought struck her: maybe Frank has called. Maybe he's fine and left a message!

"Jennifer!" Jennifer turned toward Vicky.

"Are you okay?" Vicky gasped at Jennifer's swollen eyes in her soot- smudged face.

Jennifer couldn't answer; she just wanted to get to the answering machine. Bolting from the car, she ran inside and saw on the answering machine: 4.

There were 4 messages!

CHAPTER 12

Covered in dust, Jennifer plopped down on her sofa. The answering machine was blinking 4. She took a deep breath as tears streamed down her face. "Please be Frank." She hit the play button and encircled her arms around a pillow.

"First message 8:55 a.m.," a familiar voice announced. "Frank, this is Karl. They just showed on the news that one of the Twin Towers was hit by a plane. It was the North tower. I don't know if you're headed that way, but you may want to call and reschedule your interview. They are probably going to evacuate both towers, I would think. Well, call me, so I know you're okay. 'Bye."

Jennifer could no longer see through her tears. "Please be Frank," she repeated.

"Second message 9:30 a.m." The same voice reiterated, "Frank, this is Karl. Um, the second tower….um…I'm really worried about you. Give me a call as soon as you get in. Jennifer, if you get this first, call me."

"Please be Frank," she gasped. "Please, God, be Frank or David."

"Third message 9:42 a.m." Another voice came on. "Hi, this is Rich. Two planes hit the towers, and another crashed into the Pentagon. I know Frank said something about an interview today. Well… call me." Click.

"God, please!" Tears were streaming down her face.

"Fourth message 10:32 a.m.," a different voice spoke. "Frank, this is Charlie. Um, I had a lot to drink last night, but I think I remember you saying something about an interview in the Twin Towers. I was watching the news and both towers collapsed. It looks like we're at war. Man! Give me a call as soon as you get home. And… Jennifer… I know she works near the towers so if you get this message, call me. I'm worried about you guys."

The last message hit her harder than a knife through the chest. Turning onto her side, she wept in her pillow, coughing and gasping.

Just then the phone rang.

She sat up and reached out to pick it up. Somehow, she couldn't do it. What if it was Karl, or Charlie, or someone else. How could she explain her husband might be missing?

"You've reached Frank & Jennifer's," Frank's voice announced from the black box. "We're not home right now so please leave a message, and we'll get back to you as soon as we can." Beep!

"Hi, Frank, this is Jack. I'm sorry to hear that you weren't feeling well today. Because of the events we are sending employees home to be with their families. In fact, I thought it best no one comes in until next week. Give me a call. I am just checking to make sure everyone is accounted for. Thanks, 'bye."

"Oh my God!" Jennifer cried.

She glanced to her window where she witnessed the mushrooming cloud of smoke that covered New York City. She grabbed the remote off the side table and clicked on the TV. Then she surfed the channels; news appeared on every station, and every single channel showed graphic pictures of New York. She stopped on the only one that displayed a view of a plane crashed in a field.

"This is Dave Lanson at WLBS News. At 10:42 we just got word that this flight heading from Newark, New Jersey, United Airlines Flight 93, we're told heading to San Franciso, has crashed in Somerset County, Pennsylvania. According to the FAA, this plane was also highjacked and possibly on route to the White House. The FAA believes several passengers overtook the highjackers. Back to you, Jim."

"What is happening?" Jennifer lay back down; she couldn't watch another plane with more people dead. She cried out, "What is happening? My God, what is happening?"

Just then a knock pounded on the door. She didn't get up to answer.

Both Dave and Frank knew where the extra key was above the door. "Jennifer? Jennifer?"

Jennifer couldn't get up. It was if a giant weight lay across her chest. She heard another voice, a male voice. "Is she in there?"

"She was covered in something white," Jennifer heard Vicky say. "And she won't answer. She might be hurt."

"Jennifer, this is Rich from next door. Is everything okay?"

For long minutes she lay there. She heard the TV, she heard the door knocks, but she couldn't move. All she could hear was her breathing and feel the tears streaming down her face.

CHAPTER 13

Although she could hear the TV, she no longer listened. Jennifer lay on the sofa and turned to read the clock on the phone "12:45."

More tears flowed. She knew that Frank should have been home already. He had promised to meet her for lunch. If nothing were wrong, he would have been there by now.

What would life be without him or her brother?

She remembered their wedding day three years earlier. As she stared through the veil, the door to the dressing room opened. David was standing in a tux with his elbow out. Shaking, she grabbed his arm, thankful he accepted to walk her down the aisle since their father had passed years before. He looked so dashing in a tux, tugging at the collar as if he were uncomfortable.

While the bride's music began playing, the families in the church stood. From the front the minister smiled. Frank, Karl, Charlie and Rich stood beside Frank. Her three bridesmaids, her three best friends (Suzie, Mindy, Natalie and Aunt Sophie) waited on the other side in royal turquoise dresses.

Frank stared at her with red adoring eyes, she remembered. It was the only time she ever saw him shed a tear.

After walking her down the aisle, Dave stopped beside Frank. "Who gives the bride to her groom?"

"Her brother." David leaned down and kissed her cheek, then moved her hand to Frank's. He gave Frank a quick pat on the shoulder and turned to sit in the front pew of the church.

Jennifer looked up into Frank's face; for a moment she wondered if this was the right thing to do. Would they be together for the rest of their lives?

If only she had known then how wonderful their marriage would become. She wouldn't have been afraid then; no, she would have enjoyed every second of the miracle that it was.

She heard a key going into the front door, and the knob move. Jennifer sat up. "Frank!"

In came Aunt Sophie. "The police evacuated us," she said. "I came as quickly as I could."

Jennifer heard more footsteps. Behind her, Rich, Karl and Vicky hurried in the living room.

"You okay, Jen?" Rich sat next to her.

"I still don't know where Frank is," she almost wailed.

"I'm sure he's fine," Karl responded. "You want me to make you a sandwich, or get you some water?"

Jennifer nodded no.

Aunt Sophie messed with her hair. Dust flew in every direction. "Let's get you in the shower!"

"I'm fine!"

Aunt Sophie grabbed her arm and pulled her towards the bathroom. "Karl, make her something for lunch. Vicky, your name is Vicky, right?"

"Yes."

"Find Jennifer some clothes in the closet. Rich, you try calling the hospitals while I help my niece get clean."

The group scattered as Aunt Sophie pulled her into the bathroom. Aunt Sophie leaned over and turned on the shower sprayer, testing the water. Jennifer caught a glimpse of her reflection in the mirror. Her face and clothes were tear stained and covered in white ash.

"What do you think this is, cement? What is this?" She touched her face. "Powdered glass?"

Aunt Sophie began undoing her apron. When she was done, she removed the rest of Jennifer's clothes and then pointed to the shower. "Come on, Sweetie, you must look wonderful when Frank gets home."

Jennifer knew Frank might not be coming home… that David may not be either.

Slowly, she pulled her trembling frame under the water. She felt the dirt and ash clump down her body. She hadn't taken such a bath since she was a child and used to play making dirt sand pies.

She took the bar soap, but the ash seemed to sting her body. Suddenly realizing human parts may be mixed in the ash, she started to cry again.

"I'm going to shut this door and wait in the bedroom." Aunt Sophie left her alone.

Feeling the water continue to stream down her body, Jennifer picked up the shampoo and began to wash her hair. The powder stuck together even in her hair. She lathered and rinse. With one foot out, she stepped out and turned off the tub faucet.

The door inched open, and a hand thrust in the bathroom, Vicky's hand holding a single red dress. She recognized the ring. Larry! Oh, my goodness, Larry!

Suddenly Jennifer had a flashback; one of the police cars rolling past her had the number 412 on the side! Wasn't that Larry's police car?

Jennifer dried herself with a towel and threw the dress on over her head. She took her brush off the sink and opened the bedroom door. Vicky was standing in front of her.

"Aunt Sophie is washing the white off your sofa."

"I don't give a damn about my furniture. Have you talked to Larry today?" Jennifer asked.

"He's off from work. He went to play golf this morning."

Jennifer took a deep breath. "Good. I must have read wrong… that's good."

"Let me get your hair." Vicky took the brush. "You've got a lot of knots. You know, I used to be a hair stylist before I met my first husband."

Jennifer didn't want small talk. She stood and the brush stuck in her hair. She grabbed it and quickly pulled down, ripping some of her hair out.

"Here's a hotdog," Karl came over with a plate with two hot dogs on buns. On them were cheese, relish and ketchup. "You like, cheese and relish, right? I remember from the ballpark when we all went to see the Yankees play."

"That was a good game," Rich commented.

"Yeah," Karl said.

Jennifer could tell they were trying to remain positive, but in their voices, she could hear fear. "You all can go. I'm sure Frank will be back soon. It was probably hard to get a taxi with all that going on."

"Good news." Rich hung up the phone. "No one who couldn't give a name has showed up at one hospital. Frank's not there."

"Eat, dear," Aunt Sophie said.

Jennifer lifted the hotdog up to her lips but couldn't seem to open her mouth. She stared at her hand. It was shaking. No matter how hard she tried to steady it, it trembled.

Aunt Sophie took the hot dog from her. "It's okay, dear. I'm sure..." She suddenly burst out into tears. "I'm sure he's okay. They're both okay."

Jennifer laid her head on her aunt's shoulder. No matter how hard she tried, she couldn't stop her tears. Her Aunt held her, rocking her as if she were a child.

CHAPTER 14

For quite some time Jennifer wept in her aunt's arms while the others watched television. Every channel replayed the planes hitting the Twin Towers & the Pentagon as disturbing stories unfolded about the Pennsylvania horrific plane crash.

The phone rang.

Jennifer jumped. "Frank!"

Karl stumbled and picked up the receiver. "Hello?"

"Who is it?" Jennifer quickly asked him.

Slowly, Karl lowered the receiver to his chest. "It's Drew."

Jennifer didn't know what to tell her brother's lover, but she knew he had a right to know. Her brother would have wanted it that way. Shaking, she stood and took the phone.

"Drew?"

"Thank God," came a worried voice. "I haven't heard from Dave since this morning. I've been calling the station; no answer. I mean I'm sure he has his hands full with everything going on. I went to his apartment to wait for him, and he hasn't shown up yet. I know he was supposed to get off this afternoon. Have you seen him?" Drew took a long breath. "I know. I know. He's probably out saving lives and I shouldn't be so worried and selfish."

Jennifer couldn't speak. It felt as if a frog had crawled up her throat and taken residence.

"He came home in such a good mood last night. David and Frank were getting along so well. He said Frank even believed him now that he had won another hand."

Jennifer smiled. "David did have a wonderful time last night."

"Well, I hate cards myself, but he's always trying to look good in your husband's eyes."

Jennifer sniffled. "Drew, I have to tell you something."

"This sounds serious."

"Frank was in the northern most tower being interviewed this morning by Hartman & Smith P.A.. He hasn't come home either."

Drew gasped. "I'll leave a note for David that I'm coming over to your house."

"There's more," Jennifer said.

"More?"

"David went in after Frank. He was headed into the tower. He told me to drive home. On the way, that's when the tower fell."

The phone hit the floor from Drew's end. "Drew?"

The phone was picked up. "Did you just tell me David went into the tower right before it collapsed?"

Jennifer started to cry.

"Please, tell me you didn't say that."

"I'm sorry," Jennifer mumbled. "I thought you should know. I'm scared to death for Frank too. I hope that they are together and that they found a way out before."

"I'm going to go down to the fire station to see if anyone's heard from David."

"You shouldn't go down there, Drew. The ash is very thick. It's hard to breathe."

After a long pause, "Well if you hear from either of them, call me. I'm going to stay here until Dave comes home."

"Do you want me to come over? I don't think you should be alone," Jennifer said.

"No, I just need some time here. I just need..."

"Let me know the moment you hear anything, Drew."

"Trust me, girl, I'll be screaming from the highest mountain my man is superman. I'm sure he's fine and he's out saving lives, including Frank's right now. You know there was time after the planes hit so maybe they are okay and just can't call. It did say on the news that the phone lines are down all over the city."

"Yes, that's true."

"I'll talk to you soon, okay?"

"Thanks." Jennifer hung up the phone.

Aunt Sophie leaned back against the couch, locked her fingers and prayed for several minutes. She then crossed herself and looked up. "I don't understand what Dave sees in Drew."

"He loves Drew," Jennifer said and sniffled.

Aunt Sophie gasped. "Well, I just never saw it, growing up, that he would go out with that type."

"Let's not bring this up now." Jennifer stood. "My brother could be dead because he wanted to save Frank who acts just like you about then!" Jennifer stood. "I don't want to discuss this until I know they're okay."

"Well, it's not that I don't love him," Aunt Sophie said.

Jennifer went to the kitchen, picked up the plate of hotdogs and began to eat. Through the window she saw a taxi coming down the road, covered in ash. "Taxi!" She dropped the plate and ran for the door. Everyone ran up behind her as the taxi slowly came to a stop in front of her driveway.

"It's a taxi!" Jennifer opened the door.

"I can't see who is inside," Karl said.

"Can you see through the ash?"

"No, me either," Vicky said.

"Please be Frank or David," Aunt Sophie said.

In the distance the city skyline of New York City, where once mighty buildings rose to the heavens, now showed only billowing gray smoke. Jennifer smelled the thick, choking air. She stepped out onto the porch, her eyes fixed on the back of the ash-covered taxi.

CHAPTER 15

The moment a foot hit the pavement; Jennifer started running. She recognized Frank's shoe. He exited with blood dripping down the sleeve of his ash covered suit. With tears streaming down her face, Jennifer embraced him.

"Frank!" Aunt Sophie cheered.

"Thank God!" Rich yelled from the porch. "You're alive!"

Frank lifted one arm and hugged her as tightly as he could. "I'm fine, Honey," he said, as if trying to convince himself.

She wrapped her arms around him and gave him a kiss. "I thought you were missing or worse!" She noticed his arm. "Are you all right?"

"Something hit me. I don't know, I started running and didn't stop." Frank started swaying up the driveway.

"You've lost a lot of blood." Rich checked the jacket sleeve.

"It's just a cut."

Aunt Sophie opened the door. Frank leaned down on the sofa, uncaring of the trickles of red dripping all over the leather.

"Let's see if we can take the jacket off and take a better look," Rich said.

Slowly Rich helped Frank off with his suit jacket. His white designer shirt from his shoulder down was covered in blood. Rich ripped the buttons and gently began removing it from the right side. When the left side fell, it revealed a slash from the shoulder halfway to his elbow.

"Something sharp must have hit you."

"Glass," Frank sighed, "it flew everywhere."

"We need to get you to the hospital. I'll get some bandages to stop the bleeding. I'll be right back." Rich rushed out.

"You don't know how scared I was. Did David find you?" Jennifer's face lit up. "Is he okay too?"

Frank took a deep breath. "The whole way downstairs all I thought about was you. The firefighters were in a line going up as we were coming down. They told us not to panic, keep right and not stop. Some were wearing masks. One grabbed me and it was Dave. He said that you were already on your way home." Frank started to get choked up. "I begged him to come with me, but he patted my shoulder and kept stepping higher. I watched him for a while until someone pushed me from behind. Somehow, I managed to get out of the stairwell. A cop told me to run, and I did with a bunch of people. I heard a thundering noise. I looked back and the building was falling." Frank started to tear. "There's no way Dave couldn't have gotten out. It happened so fast. Maybe he's alive, somewhere. I don't know."

Jennifer reached out and held Frank. The world that once seemed okay quickly turned to pain. "David got out! I'm sure. You'll see."

Rich hurried to the floor and began wrapping up Frank's arm. "We got to get Frank to a hospital. He's losing a lot of blood."

"Why didn't you go to the doctors first?" Jennifer asked.

Frank sighed, heavily. "I just wanted to come home."

Rich grabbed Frank and pulled him to his feet. "Let's go, Buddy, we don't have time to waste."

Aunt Sophie said, "Let's all take him."

"My parents' car is out front," Rich said.

Jennifer slipped into the backseat while Rich helped Frank into the passenger side of the front. Then, he sat behind the wheel of the town car. They headed towards the billowing smoke which once was the skyline of their most beloved city, forever changed.

"My God!" Frank gasped, seeing the new skyline for the first time. "Look what they've done!"

Rich spoke coldly. "War."

CHAPTER 16

As the group hurried into the hospital, they were surrounded by dozens of white coated medical personnel. "Right here." A large woman led Frank toward a bed. "We'll take your insurance information in a minute."

Jennifer followed. Aunt Sophie and Rich kept pace behind her, as they walked down the hallway and into the room. Jennifer saw the surgeon who had fixed Frank's knee two years ago and waved.

A tall man wearing a "Dr. Rogers" nametag rushed over and helped Frank sit on the bed. Gently, he removed Franks's shirt and began examining the cut.

"Have you been dizzy at all?" he asked. "Feeling faint?"

"Not really," Frank hissed.

The doctor landed a stethoscope on his chest. "Cold," Frank complained.

Jennifer sat down on a chair by the bed. Rich and Aunt Sophie stood near the back wall, trying to keep out of the doctor's way. "Do you think I'll need stitches?" Frank questioned.

"We'll run some tests. Looks like a few dozen of those." Frank nodded.

"You want help, Dr. Rogers?" A nurse shifted the curtain further open.

"Cleanse this wound." He started walking for the door. "I need the patient down in X-ray as soon as possible."

"Right away."

Jennifer noticed several nurses standing in the hall. She clicked open her purse and stood. "I got our insurance card. Who do I talk to?"

"I'll get someone," a young woman said and scurried off.

"My Goodness," Aunt Sophie said. "I've been to this hospital many times and never got service like this."

"You'd think they'd be packed," Rich said.

A tall, ebony female entered, wearing a navy business suit. "We were earlier right after the towers fell," she said. "Are you with the patient? I'm Laurie from administration. Do you have your insurance card?"

"Here it is." Jennifer handed it to her.

"Are you his wife?"

Tears filled Jennifer's eyes as she barely was able to voice the word, "Still."

The woman seemed to know what she meant by that and smiled. "Fill out these forms and I'll be right back."

Jennifer took the clip board and recognized the address form from when Frank had been treated for the motorcycle accident.

A tear ran down her cheek as she looked down at the lines. She had been so mad about him buying a motorcycle; she begged him to get rid of it. How silly that fight seemed now. He had loved that bike and always wore a helmet. She decided right then to buy him another.

"You want me to fill this out?" Frank asked her.

Aunt Sophie took it from Jennifer. "You've been through enough today."

"Thanks." Jennifer reached down in her purse and grabbed a pen. Aunt Sophie quickly took it from her.

"I'm fine," Frank said.

Jennifer wiped her eyes. "I know."

The first nurse came back with a wheelchair. "I'm going to take you to cleanse that wound and then to X-ray. Have a seat."

Frank hopped out of bed and sat down.

"Your husband will be back in about 30 minutes," the nurse informed. Another woman in scrubs moved forward. "I'll help."

Jennifer watched Frank being wheeled down the hall. She then crossed to the nurse's station. "Do you have a list of people who came in today?"

"I'll check the database. Are you missing someone?"

"My brother David Rivers; he's a firefighter."

The nurse moved over to a computer and typed something in. "I'm sorry he's not at this hospital. With everything that's happening, he's probably helping."

"I know," Jennifer nodded.

"Would you like to see a doctor?" she asked. "We can give you something to calm your nerves."

"No, that's okay."

"Were you there?" Dr. Rogers came from behind and asked.

"I'm fine. I'm just concerned for Frank."

"Hopefully he will just need stitches." The doctor smiled. "Well, if you change your mind. I'd be happy to prescribe something."

"Thank you, but I'm okay. I'll just go back and wait for my…" she got choked up, "husband."

"Lisa," the doctor said to the nurse to his right. "Why don't you get her and her friends something to drink?"

Lisa asked Jennifer, "Would you like sodas?"

"That's very kind of you."

"Take the drinks into the room. It's fine for today," the doctor said. Lisa scurried off.

"I'll help." Another nurse followed.

Jennifer commented, "I've never seen so many doctors or nurses before."

"They all came in off the clock."

Jennifer understood. "So many?"

"Only two on the hospital's entire staff didn't come in to volunteer," Dr. Rogers said. "The sad part is we had a major rush right after it happened, and a few serious cases moved to ICU, but other than that, it's slower than usual. We were all hoping that we could have helped more."

"Really?"

"None of the staff left either. I tried about an hour ago but I kept wondering what if they bring in more." The doctor grimaced. "I'm sorry your brother is missing. He's probably saving lives right now."

"I hope so," Jennifer replied.

"Well, let me know if I can help you further. I'll be here."

Jennifer went back to her room but before she even sat on her chair, Lisa and her friend returned to the floor with several cans.

Aunt Sophie took a can and gulped down the liquid contents. "That hit the spot."

Rich took a soda for himself.

Lisa handed Jennifer one, and as she did Jennifer stood and hugged her. "Only water and juice for me, but thanks anyway."

Surprised, Lisa hugged her back. "Thank you." "Thanks for being here just in case."

Lisa nodded. "I hope you find your brother soon."

"Me too…" Jennifer sat down and looked back up to the clock. In less than thirty minutes she'd see Frank again and she couldn't wait to lay her eyes on him again, alive.

CHAPTER 17

Being pushed by a nurse, Frank reentered the hospital room on a wheelchair. "I'll be fine. The doctor checked X-rays. There's no break and my blood work looks good. He wrote me this prescription." He handed a piece of paper to Jennifer. "It's antibiotics, a few days worth just to make sure an infection doesn't set in. And I might have to come back to get the stitches out." He began rising from the wheelchair.

"Hospital policy requires you remain in the chair," the nurse began pushing him back into the hall, "and the stitches dissolve by themselves."

Frank muttered, "They've come a long way from when I was a kid, Jen."

Jennifer, Rich, and Aunt Sophie followed Frank out of the hospital. Rich ran for the car as the nurse waited to reclaim the wheelchair. A few minutes later, Rich drove up and the group got into the car with Frank sitting in the passenger's side.

"Let's get you home," Jennifer said and sighed. "I want to check the messages to see if David called."

Frank glanced to the back seat over his shoulder. "We have to talk to Drew, Honey."

Knowing Frank didn't care for Drew, Jennifer suggested, "I think we should go home."

Frank insisted. "Rich, drive us to Drew's apartment first."

"You sure you're up for that," Karl questioned.

Frank nodded yes. After negotiating several smoke filled streets and crossing over the railroad tracks, the car parked below a twenty story apartment building.

Immediately, Frank climbed out of the car and the group headed to the elevator.

"Maybe David's here," Jennifer said.

For a brief moment, she thought of the Twin Towers and how that had been an easy target for an airplane. For the first time in her life, she worried about going up in a tall building. Her heart began to pound. She shook off the horrible feeling just as the elevator doors opened and the group rose to the 8th floor apartment marked 849.

Frank knocked.

The door flew open. A smile came. He crinkled his glasses in front of giant blue eyes.

"Hi, Drew," Frank greeted. "Can we come in?"

A short, stocky man with a shaved head looked over Frank's arm. "Are you okay? Come right in."

"I'm fine." Frank moved past Drew and entered the living room.

Jennifer glanced over the eclectic room filled with classic pieces such as Ernest Hemmingway furniture. Fine art by Vincent Van Gogh, David Bromstad, Picasso and Barbara Lossman hung on the walls. The 60-inch plasma television was turned on to a news station. Frank reached for the remote and turned it off. Jennifer sat down next to him as Aunt Sophie and Rich sat at the adjacent dining room table.

"Can I get anyone a drink?" Drew offered.

"Have you heard from David?" Jennifer questioned.

"No, but I'm sure with everything going on he's very busy," Drew said. "Would anyone care for a snack?"

Frank nodded no. "You need to sit down, Drew. I have something to tell you."

"Don't!" Jennifer said, not wanting to hear Frank's story again.

"What is it?" Drew sat down on the block multi-colored recliner.

"I was going down the stairwell of one of the towers when I saw David. He told me Jennifer was waiting for me at home. He kept climbing up and when I got to the bottom, not long after, the building collapsed."

The smile melted off of Drew's face.

"David still could have gotten out," Jennifer said. "Frank might not have seen him."

"True," Frank said and sighed. "But I thought you should know what I saw, and I know he means a lot to you. And…" Frank stopped himself. "I just wanted to tell you in person."

Frank rose and walked to the phone. Next to it was an address book and he flipped through the pages. Suddenly, he stopped and dialed a number. He put the receiver to his ear.

"Hi, this is Frank, Jennifer's husband. I would really appreciate it if you would come over here."

A female voice was heard mumbling back.

"Yes, I saw David in the first building right before it went down and well, I don't want Drew to be alone right now. Can you come?" Frank hung up the phone. "Your mom and sister are on their way, Drew."

Jennifer turned to Drew who was now in tears. She looked away to the picture on the wall. It was of her brother and Drew, their arms wrapped around each other.

Drew gasped. "Are you telling me David's dead, Frank?"

Frank kneeled down beside him and put his arm on his shoulder. "I know you loved him, Drew." Drew whimpered as Frank stood uneasily and motioned Jennifer to follow.

Aunt Sophie rose. "I'll stay until his family arrives," she said to Rich. "Make sure Jen & Frank get home safely."

Rich nodded and followed Jennifer and Frank to the door. On the way, he patted Drew on the back. "Don't lose faith, Bro, the firefighters are finding survivors."

Frank shook his head for Rich to shut up. Rich then moved to the door after Frank and Jen. Jennifer looked one last time at Drew. Her heart was breaking for his pain.

Frank murmured, "His mom and sister will be here soon. Don't worry, Honey."

"I should stay," Jennifer responded. "We're his family, too."

"Jen, you need to rest."

CHAPTER 18

Clinging onto hope, as she watched a fire truck drive past, Jennifer raised her poster which read, "Have you seen my brother?" Pasted below was a picture of David in firefighter uniform.

Surrounding her were dozens of people clasping their own signs. Some taped their photos to lampposts. Most stood hour after hour, their sole desire any news on their missing loved ones.

When night fell, she pulled away, got behind the wheel of her ash-covered car and drove home. Frank didn't say a word as she entered. He watched her get into bed, and then climbed in next to her. She didn't feel like talking. His arm went underneath her pillow as he rolled over onto his side, facing her.

"Try to sleep tonight," he encouraged.

For the next several minutes she listened to his breathing. Covering herself with a soft cotton blanket, she heard a voice coming from the side of the bed, "Jen."

She rolled over and discovered a firefighter jacket around giant shoulders of a shiny male form. There wasn't a spot of ash on it. As if new, dark and glistening, the jacket adorned bright yellow letters, FDNY. She glanced up and saw familiar sea blue gems. "David?"

"You know I would have called by now if I was okay." A glowing hand reached down and lay on top of hers. She felt warmth but not the fingers. "They found my ring. Be sure to give it to him." David's figure began to fade and then before disappearing, said, "I love you, always."

"Come back!" she screamed. Her eyes fluttered open to find Frank's face inches from her own.

"You okay, Jen?" Frank shook her.

In a panic Jennifer's body flew out of the bed and started looking around the bedroom. She searched over the dresser and the side tables; no one was there. "David? David?"

"It was a dream, Jen, a nightmare." Frank pulled her gently back down on the bed. "Get back to sleep."

A knock came from the front of the house.

"I'll get rid of whoever it is." Frank jumped up, hurried into the living room and opened the door.

Jennifer could see that it was someone in a firefighter uniform. She rushed out of the bedroom and came forward. "David?"

When she got to the doorway, she discovered a man over six feet six. His sunken eyes were filled with sorrow. Around his neck was a crucifix, silver, and made to appear as large nails of the cross. His hands were shaking, and he leaned heavily on one leg.

"Hi, Frank," his deep voice greeted, "I'm Robbie Benson. I've worked with David for the past four years. I think we met a long time ago at a Christmas party."

"I don't remember you," Jennifer said.

He leaned his giant frame further onto one side, scratching his rough beard. Then he put a hand into his dirty ash-covered fireman jacket. "I wanted to come personally."

"Jen, get back to the bed," Frank insisted.

"Do you have news on my brother, Mr. Benson?" she said and gasped.

"David was in a tower as it collapsed."

"We know," Jennifer said. "Please get back to ground zero and find him."

His sad eyes trailed to hers. He didn't utter a word for quite some time, until finally he pulled out a hand with a silver ring, and muttered very softly, "We did."

"Is he okay?" Jennifer wailed.

"Some of the guys sang, 'God bless America,' others saluted as we moved him into the ambulance. What was left was taken to the city morgue where arrangements can be made."

Frank grabbed Jen as she screamed in horror.

"There are many families that won't get even that," Robert informed.

"You're lying!" Jennifer cried. "My brother's not dead!"

"His arm had his unit number and name on it. He was wearing this," Robert said and raised the simple silver band with the claddagh Irish symbol. "He told me once it was Drew and his wedding ring even though they wore them on their right hands. I thought Drew would want it back. Please let us know when the funeral is; our ladder company will be there."

Jennifer placed her head onto Frank's shoulder, but it granted no comfort. She couldn't believe what she just heard. This stranger who she swore she had never met before was telling her that her own flesh and blood, her only sibling, was dead. This seemed more like a nightmare than the one she just had. David had just been there beside her bed, touching her hand. That had been real, hadn't it? "This can't be!"

Frank took the ring. In the palm of his hand, the silver band sparkled. He clasped it in his fingers, holding it tightly.

"The city is taking volunteers now to help dig so if we're not working, we're supervising. But we'll all go to David's funeral."

"I'll find out when Drew wants to hold the service and then contact the station," Frank said.

"Would you like me to tell Drew?"

"I will," Frank said, softly.

"Thank you." A wave of relief moved across Robert's large features. He turned, favoring the right leg, and hobbled down the front porch steps, donning his firefighter helmet.

After shutting the door, Frank swept Jennifer up into his arms and carried her back to bed. He placed her gently on the blanket where she wept into her pillow, her hands gripping both ends.

For several minutes Frank didn't speak. He sat down beside her. Softly rubbing her back, fighting his own tears, he said, "Drew needs to know, Jen. I'll call Aunt Sophie and wait until she gets here before I go."

"Why my brother? Why out of all the firefighters in the world, why him?" Her eyes reflected his, filled with overwhelming grief.

He answered simply, "Why anybody?"

CHAPTER 19

Jennifer crawled out of bed achingly ill from head to toe, with her body trembling, her head pounding. Hearing the television on in the other room, she slowly rose and noticed Aunt Sophie in the recliner, her hand clutching the remote.

On the TV, Mayor Giuliani had his hands up, praising the people of New York for their bravery in this time of crisis in their city.

An African American man about mid-sixties replaced the Mayor at the podium. There were wrinkles around his mouth, deepening as he uttered in a dark, deep, and clear voice, "My fellow Americans, between the Atlantic and the Pacific oceans, they can bomb our cities, but they can never take away what has built this country and made it what it is today. This country stands for every man, woman, and child. No matter the wealth, race, religion, sexual preference, education, size or abilities of each individual. We are a people who overcome differences because we are just that, Americans, protecting our rights and our freedoms so that those who threaten us will never take away our united greatness."

The crowd erupted in massive cheer.

Worried about the sudden noise, Aunt Sophie lowered the volume and checked. Discovering Jennifer awake, she hurried to the bedroom, tears coming to her eyes. "I can hardly believe it."

"I know."

"Frank hasn't returned," Aunt Sophie announced. "He was at David's all night with Drew. He called this morning to tell me that Rich and he are helping Drew make arrangements."

"Is Drew's mother there?"

Aunt Sophie nodded. "I talked with her on the phone and their whole family is just devastated."

Jennifer pointed to one of the pictures on the nightstand. Among a few of Frank and her was one of Drew. Clutched in his hand was a shiny round bronze disk hanging off of a red, blue and white necklace. "When Drew went to the Olympics, I met her. Barbara wore flags all in her hair and clothes that were all red, white and blue. The whole time Drew skated to show tunes, she didn't even look on the ice; she prayed the whole time to Jesus, out loud, begging him to let Drew land a quad, whatever that was." Jennifer let herself smile. "When he won the bronze, she started crying and David, I'd never seen him so proud."

"We're going to make it through this together," Aunt Sophie said.

The doorbell rang and Aunt Sophie answered. From the bedroom, Jennifer could see a man in a plain brown uniform holding a silver vase of flowers. He didn't look up when he asked, "Jennifer?"

"No, that's my niece. Are these for her?"

"Sign here." He held out a clipboard.

Her Aunt signed and he handed her a vase full of red roses.

Jennifer grabbed her purse and moved to stand beside her aunt. "Beautiful." She smelled them and noticed the man appeared tired, slumped over and breathing slow as if trying to take a break. "Thank you for the delivery." She handed him five dollars.

He stuffed the bill in his shirt pocket. "Do you know where number 1100 is?"

"Across the street." Aunt Sophie nodded to the larger house with tinted green shutters and the giant red maple tree in the center of the leaf-covered yard.

Jennifer asked, surprised, "You have flowers for Victoria Martin too?"

"I've been delivering flowers in this neighborhood ever since the terrorist attack. If it was Bin Laden, I hope they stuff him like the pig."

Jennifer ignored the comment. "Have you delivered to 1100 before?"

"My partner did. He said it was right by yours and gave me the directions. Your house has a set of carnations coming after lunch. We're completely out so we have to wait until our supplier arrives this afternoon."

Aunt Sophie placed the vase on a table and checked the small white card. She read, "My heart is with you always, Drew."

The stranger turned on a heel and headed to the van with, "A.L.K. Flowers Inc," on the side. He slid open the door and pulled out a plant in a big oriental painted pot. About two feet tall, the leafy house fern had curly ends clumping together.

Jennifer realized the driver must have been hearing death sentiments all day, knowing that those getting the flowers had loved ones gone. No wonder he appeared so tired.

As the man headed across the street, Jennifer followed. She opened the door before he even rang the doorbell. Victoria Martin who usually dressed to the nines wasn't wearing her normal fancy outfits or smelling of her favorite perfume; she stood slumped over in a plain cotton robe. Her face wore no makeup. Her eyes shined bright red as if she had been crying non-stop.

Vicky handed the delivery driver a bill. He switched it for the fern and then went back into his truck without uttering a word.

With tears falling down her pale cheeks, she looked up to Jennifer, placed the plant down and embraced her. In each other's arms they held one another, neighbor to neighbor.

"I'm so sorry about David," Vicky said. "Rich told me."

Jennifer didn't even need to ask to know why she was having deliveries too.

"I'm so sorry."

"I loved Gary!" Vicky cried. "I can't believe he's dead."

"Are they sure?" Jennifer asked.

"Yes… his partner…"

Jennifer nodded, not wanting to hear the gruesome details.

Vicky began, saying, "He saw Gary and an old woman by the tower. He was helping her into their police car, to drive her to safety. Then the building fell. They didn't have any time. Ron, that's his partner, said he barely even made it out alive himself and he was half down the street helping another victim."

"I'm so sorry."

"Look at all these flowers." Vicky opened the door and there were dozens of bushels, plants and baskets of fruit lining the richly decorated entrance. "I even got two casseroles in my fridge from the family who lives around the corner."

"It doesn't help." Jennifer knew.

Suddenly a black SUV Drew barreled down the street with Frank behind the wheel. He drove into their driveway across the road and walked over to the front steps. There Aunt Sophie and Frank stood, watching them.

"You better get home to your husband."

"I'll stay."

Vicky shook her head no. "Be with your husband, enjoy every minute. You hear me, every second!"

Jennifer gave her one last hug. She waited until Vicky shut the door and then hurried across the grass to a man with a heavy-laden heart worn all over his expressive dark face.

CHAPTER 20

The sweet smell of the roses engulfed her senses as Jennifer entered her home after Frank and Aunt Sophie. She stared at the lovely blooms, recalling how many flowers were tossed over the ice years ago.

Wanting to relive happier moments, she went to the DVD player, grabbed a DVD marked 1998 Olympics, pressed it in and punched the play button. While Aunt Sophie and Frank went into the kitchen, she moved to sit on the sofa.

"What are you putting in?" Frank asked.

"What about the news?" Aunt Sophie questioned.

"I'll turn it back on in a minute," Jennifer replied.

The screen darkened with copyright laws then flashed to a rink with 5 circles of different colors designed below the ice. In the center stood Drew, wearing tight black pants, a flowing white shirt and a shiny pair of leather ice skates. Thousands in attendance surrounded the rink, their attention locked on him.

A show tune began, and big band sounds carried throughout the packed auditorium as Drew glided forward. The audience grew silent, dazzled by his precise movements. When the music sped up, he did too, electrifyingly, becoming an artistic spectacle masterpiece.

"He's rocking the house," Frank noted.

"Drew is amazing," Aunt Sophie reflected, wryly. "He began at age six!"

The television announcer pointed out, "And there's Drew's mother." The camera shifted to a woman wearing a big red, white and blue coat.

Her hands were clasped together, praying. Her eyes closed tight as if she was not able to watch. Next to her was David, his teeth clenched, his eyes targeted on Drew. Seeing her brother again with his piercing blue eyes filled with hope, Jen felt both pain and joy simultaneously.

The camera returned to the ice as Drew skated his first combination. He twirled in the air and landed perfectly, as if it were easy.

The crowd exploded with applause. The music meter changed when drums pounded as if at war. With perfect precision, Drew changed into faster footwork and crosscut the ice.

"Drew has just completed a Triple Axle and Triple Toe jump with extraordinary footwork. His next move should be the Triple Lutz, and the gold will be his!" the announcer cried out.

Drew was putting emotion and soul into this performance, thought Jennifer. He turned into position, jumped again, but couldn't pull off the last landing. His hand shot down to avoid falling, his fingers drawing up splashes of ice.

"That will cost him against the Russian Magoza who has yet to skate," the announcer predicted.

Drew's face glowed as he continued as if on fire. The song couldn't contain his magnificence as he leapt into a death drop and spun onto one foot. Leaning over, his head touched one knee for a few seconds, then he lowered the leg, spinning in place. The twirling started slow but built fast and furiously like a whirling dervish. Then in an instant, he raised his arms out just as the music ended with a loud finale.

The crowd jumped to their feet. With a crinkled, pleased face, Drew's eyes filled with tears.

"He should have won gold," Aunt Sophie opined.

"No matter what those judges say, he shined tonight," announced the commentator.

Drew bowed to each side of the auditorium. Flowers rained like parade candy as he headed to a bench in front of the cameras. Waiting patiently, he wiped his face with a towel and seated himself to receive his Technical Merit and Presentation scores.

Scores of 5.8 and 5.9 posted across the scoreboard.

For presentation 6.0 from three judges, the rest awarded 5.9.

Jennifer shut off the DVD player. She didn't want to see the Russian skate the perfect 6.0. In her eyes, Drew was the most amazing male figure skater who had ever lived.

"If it weren't for that one landing, he would have been the gold medalist," Aunt Sophie murmured.

"He should do a real sport like hockey," Frank whispered then turned to the fridge for a beer.

Jennifer pulled out the DVD. "Drew's supposed to represent the USA in February at Salt Lake City in Utah. David was already planning their trip."

"He probably won't go," Aunt Sophie concluded, "if there is even going to be the Olympics."

Jennifer turned back to look at the large rose bouquet sitting on her kitchen counter. "I'm going to be in that audience if there is. That's what David would have wanted."

Aunt Sophie nodded. "You're right."

CHAPTER 21

Glued to the television to hear news on who had crashed the planes into the Twin Towers, Jennifer couldn't fathom how anyone could murder thousands of innocent women, children and men civilians. They used planes like bombs to take down American and historical landmarks. Was it truly Bin Laden and the Al Queda network?

When Saturday arrived, she slipped on a simple black dress, feeling numb. Her whole world seemed to change in an instant. She buttoned up, realizing safety was an illusion.

She pivoted from the mirror and discovered Frank dressed in a dark three-piece navy suit. His Italian nose crinkled as he finished straightening his silk white tie. With hazel eyes twinkling, he raised his large square jaw and slightly smiled with heart shaped full lips. She knew Frank forced that happy expression to cheer her, this being the dreaded day of her brother's funeral.

She could barely grasp David's untimely demise. What would her life be without him?

When they were kids in a dirt pile, their hands mixed in mud, David tossed a handful which landed in her eyes. Her tiny hands flew to her face as she cried out. Little David hurried over with the hose, watered her face until she felt no more pain. Lowering the hose, he gave her a hug and apologized. From that moment on, no matter how hard they fought, she knew he would always come to her rescue. Even at four, she counted on her older brother.

"I'll start the car," Frank announced, walking toward the garage.

Jennifer grabbed her purse and stepped outside her house. Glancing down the street, she knew America would never be the same again. The most horrific terrorist attack in human history affected more than New York City, the Pentagon, the Pennsylvania crash site and rescue personnel. It affected her and every person around America, people young and old, from all races and religions. Flags were even flying on every house down the street but not on her own.

Frank pulled the car out of the garage and asked, "What's wrong?"

 "Where's our flag?"

"I don't know."

Jennifer went into the garage, searched behind some boxes to the corner where the brooms and mops were kept. Leaning against the back of the garage was a flag rolled up on a flagpole. She began to untie it and hurried to the bracket off the front porch. Quickly she stuck the pole into its slot, and the flag unfurled in one mighty wave of the wind. The garage door began to lower, and Jennifer got into the passenger's side.

"We're going to be a few minutes late," Frank said, "especially with all the traffic."

"Drew won't let them start without us, I'm sure." Jennifer buckled her seatbelt.

"You're right," Frank agreed. "They'll be waiting on us."

As they drove down the highway, Jennifer noticed that every marquee announced, "God bless America," or "United we Stand." Cars passed them with flag stickers on the bumpers or small flags tied to antenna, even flags draped over luggage racks.

The drive felt unlike any other she had ever taken. She was a proud American before, but seeing the flags today, displayed in such diverse ways, hit her differently than on any Fourth of July or President's Day. This varied display of the colors spoke of courage and unity of billions.

As the SUV stopped at an exit red light, Jennifer heard a familiar tune drifting from a breakfast shop that had opened its doors to welcome customers. The Star-Spangled Banner blasted from a loudspeaker.

Oh, say does that star spangled banner Yet wave!

O'er the land of the free

And the home of the brave!

A chill ran down her spine. She'd heard the words a thousand times before, but this day she truly appreciated how Francis Scott Key must have felt as he wrote them. What a welcome sight is the red, white and blue banner flying high after all the US had been through. Even though the light turned green, the cars surrounding them didn't speed. The lady next to Jennifer wiped her eyes and gave her a nod before proceeding on her way.

The world become different today, Jennifer surmised. The horror meant to divide was somehow pulling everyone together. Through this tragedy, even she was becoming aware of how dedicated she was to stay an American.

The flag, once a symbol of our country, she learned in grade school rings true today as it did 224 years ago when Congress decided:

The stars represent each of the United States.

The blue field behind the stars stands for vigilance, perseverance and justice.

The white stripes reflect purity and innocence. The red stripes symbolize valor and courage.

Those terrorist were murderers for sure, but they could not kill her American spirit; if anything, her love for her country is forever strengthened.

The car pulled into the parking lot of a brick two story building labeled, "Brownie's Funeral Home." Frank drove the car into the last spot left in the back.

"We better hurry," Frank said.

"Okay," she muttered, fighting back her tears.

"You going to be all right?" he asked, slowly.

Jennifer unbuckled her seatbelt and a small smile crept across her troubled face. "You know my brother died an American hero."

Frank stopped himself from getting out, turned back and smiled. "I know, Princess."

CHAPTER 22

Soft piano music filled the funeral home as Frank and Jennifer entered the dark, candle lit room. The poker gang members proceeded quietly down the center aisle. Flower baskets surrounded a giant framed photograph of David among his ladder company in FDNY blue uniforms at the front of the room. The same firefighters in the picture filled the sixth, seventh and eighth row.

An African American woman smiled up at Jennifer. Dressed in a black suit crowned with a large, flowered hat, she was seated next to Gelsid, along with the rest of Rich's family. Rich's soon-to-be ex-wife Maria was in attenDrewce; Jennifer and Frank nodded hello to her as they approached the front to sit beside Aunt Sophie.

With his head hung low and face covered in tears, Drew entered from a side door and seated himself next to Jennifer. "Thank you for being here," he mumbled.

"Are you hanging in there?" She placed her arm around him, trying desperately not to burst into tears.

"As well as I can be today," Drew muttered. With red eyes, he attempted a stiff smile.

In front of the hall lay a long white casket with gold trim. Jennifer could hardly contemplate her brother's remains inside. Her heart longed for his voice, his hugs and those brilliant blue eyes again. Just one more time would make her the happiest sister alive. She saw the heart shaped roses on the center of the casket. "Did you send that arrangement?" she questioned Drew.

"I had them shipped in from New Jersey because so many florists were out of red," Drew proudly explained.

"Which one is ours?" Frank whispered in Jennifer's ear.

"I don't remember," she admitted. "I think I ordered lilies."

Next to the many bundles of flower arrangements and lighted candles sat a table with the words, "In my castle, there are many rooms…" engraved. A chubby man in a three-piece suit moved to the podium, put a hand through his graying hair, donned a set of reading glasses, and began to speak.

"Good morning," he greeted. "My name is Pastor Liam O'Malley. I was asked to perform David J.D. Miller's memorial service by my good friend Drewiel Fitzgerald. I don't know all of you, but I did know David, well. I begin with great sadness." He opened the black Bible on the podium.

Jennifer began feeling a lump in her throat; she coughed and opened her purse to pull out a tissue. Frank reached his hand and took one.

"David Miller died on September the 11th, a day which forever shook our nation. For years he fought fires and saved lives, never asking for appreciation. A peaceful man, supportive of Drew's skating career, and of his friends and family, his only wish was to serve humanity. So, we ask why? Why was he so brave and why is he lying here today? For us no answer will ever assuage our grief, especially for those rescued during his five years as one of New York's finest firefighters. Julia, come and tell us your story."

An older woman, heavyset, wearing a long dark dress with a large white blossom on the right side of her breast, slowly rose from a pew and walked to the podium. In a wavering voice, she announced, "My name is Julia Sellis. I live on the East side. Two years ago, I was trapped in my fiery apartment when a handsome young fellow picked me up and carried me out. I never got the chance to thank him, didn't even know his name, until I saw his picture in the obituary. Because of him

I'm still here for my great grandchildren. I came to say thanks." She touched the top of the coffin, then shuffled back behind the firefighters who loudly applauded.

When the cheers faded, the Pastor called, "Lacey, will you come forward now."

A short overweight woman hurried to the front and wiped her eyes. "Hi, my name is Jessica Lacey. I work in the Trade Center and on September the 11th, I was in my office when the plane hit. I thought the building would be fine. I was waiting by the elevator when the hall began filling with smoke. David waved me over from the stairwell. Shortly, after I escaped, the building collapsed. I have no doubt that David saved…" she began to cry, "many lives because he led many of my coworkers to the stairwell entrance."

Cheers resounded. The Pastor waited for several minutes, put his arm around her, then continued. "These are a few of whom David's helped over the years, but there was more to him than his duties. David was a good man to all who loved him, to his life partner Drew, his sister Jennifer, and the rest of his family and friends. We've joined together today to ask God to open his arms, embrace him in heaven as much as we have on earth. Let us pray."

All heads silently lowered, Jennifer wiped her eyes, realizing this was the last time she would ever be near her brother again.

"We miss our friend and our family member, Lord. Help us to understand and cherish our wonderful memories of him. We ask you to welcome his soul and bless each and every one of us, in this difficult time and our beloved country. Amen." The Pastor raised a hand, motioning the firefighters forward. "Let us bring our American hero, David J.D. Miller, to his resting place."

Eight firefighters rose and padded over to the white coffin which reflected candlelight. They raised the shining box onto their shoulders and began carrying it slowly out. The Pastor asked Jennifer, Frank, Drew, and his mother to follow.

The doors of the funeral home opened. The sky had darkened with thick black clouds and thunder clapped. Drips of rain fell on the large group opening umbrellas as the glistening casket was moved toward a tent in the distance across a grave-marked land.

The group passed four other funerals on their journey. Noting the wives, husbands and all the children, Jennifer grieved for all those forever to mourn because of a day in September that will never be forgotten.

CHAPTER 23

As the firefighters lowered the coffin into the ground, Jennifer remembered David whom she could always talk to, depend on, and love.

Gunshots rang out.

The crowd turned to another funeral to the right with dozens of uniformed police officers and a grieving widow clutching three weeping children. Jennifer turned back to look one last time at her brother's coffin. If only she had known that Frank's game would be the last she'd ever see him. She would have begged David to stay, tell him she loved him, spend so much more time with him.

The Pastor closed the notebook he had in his hand and said, "Ashes to ashes, dust to dust. May God bless all who mourn and give us strength. Amen."

"Amen." Everyone gathered above the coffin.

"Drew, would you like to say a few words," the Pastor asked.

Drew wiped his eyes and stood above the grave. "I would just like to thank you all for coming. I loved David with all my heart, and no one will ever replace him… that's really all I had to say." He took off his watch and tossed it onto the coffin. "You are all welcome to my mother's house for some drinks and food. If you need directions just let me know. Thanks again and I really appreciate your coming."

A few of the firefighters began to walk away. Rich watched Maria leave, and Jennifer couldn't help but see the heartbreak wash across his face.

"You should thank her for attending," Jennifer said to Rich.

Rich picked Gelsid up and held him close to his chest. The boy wrapped his arms around his neck. "You're right. I'll see if she needs a ride to Drew's." He immediately rushed after her.

"I can't believe my nephew's gone," Aunt Sophie mumbled.

"I know," Frank consoled.

Drew closed in. "Will you all be coming to Mother's?"

"Can I bring anything?" Jennifer asked.

Drew shook his head no. "I'd better be getting things ready."

"If you need anything, let me know," Jennifer said.

He nodded and began heading off to a group of women huddled underneath several large umbrellas.

"Do you think Drew will be all right?" Frank questioned Jennifer.

"I don't know if I'm going to be." Suddenly her eyes focused on two people walking toward the funeral, Vicky and someone straight off a music video, Rocky Peterson, the guitarist for Gypsy King. With long black hair flowing in the wind, squinting through the rain and underneath a pierced eyebrow, he came over and held out a tattooed hand for Frank to shake.

"I'm so sorry to hear about your brother-in-law," Rocky said. "I heard he was a fan from my sister who works for the police department."

Vicky smiled. "Supermodel Lenora Peterson had heard about David and Drew? Can you believe it? Rocky stopped at your house today to give his condolences and I told him about the funeral, and he wanted to come. I'm sorry we didn't get here earlier."

Jennifer could barely believe that David's favorite guitarist was standing right in front of her, someone she had seen so many times in newspapers, music videos and in rock magazines.

Vicky called to Drew, "Come and meet Rocky Peterson."

"David would be so thrilled. I mean he loved Gypsy King music..." Drew took a deep breath. "Thank you so much for coming. I'm sure he's looking down and smiling."

"You mind if I play a tune?" he asked, partly sheltered from the rain by a large tree.

Drew came over, wiping his red, swollen eyes. "Not at all!"

"What was David's favorite song by my band?"

"Ocean Waters," Jennifer answered.

Rocky went to the limousine parked in the lot and returned with an acoustic guitar strapped to his shoulder. Without even an introduction, he began to strum. Those still in attendance turned to listen to his sultry voice.

"Lone ocean waters flowing across the deep, In your waves of wisdom I learned love will keep."

After he finished, a request came in from the Reverend, "How about God bless America," he asked.

"I try never to turn down a man of the cloth," Rocky said and smirked. His full lower lip moved, and the next song radiated out, flowing out like a cool fall breeze.

The crowd didn't clap when he closed; a lull hung the air.

The musician rose then gripped Jennifer's hand, placing his on top of hers. "I am so sorry to hear about the loss of your loved one. This has been such a tragedy, but for you and Drew especially. If there is anything that Gypsy King can do for your family just let us know. We're doing a benefit concert for victims, and I'll send tickets, but if you need anything else, don't hesitate to ask."

"Thank you." Jennifer smiled.

"How kind of you to come," Drew added.

"I made plans to go to Ground Zero this afternoon. The Governor and Mayor will be there. I hope you understand that I want to tell them of the concert."

"Of course." Drew smiled.

Rocky turned to the group, briefly waved and returned to his black limousine. Jennifer watched his straight hair flowing as he put his guitar back in a leather case.

Suddenly Vicky hugged Jennifer. "I'm sorry I was late. When he showed up on your doorstep, I wanted to tell him all about David and Drew. How much we will all miss him." Her voice cracked as the coffin began lowering into a six-foot hole.

"Goodbye." Jennifer laid her head on Vicky's shoulder and burst into tears. They wept for as long as rain fell that day.

CHAPTER 24

David's friends and family packed the small apartment. Jennifer could see Aunt Sophie, Karl, Rich, Charlie, and Vicky through the doorway around a large ebony grand piano played by a man in black tuxedo.

Drew quickly greeted Frank as they entered from the elevator. Wanting privacy, Jennifer asked, "Can we speak, Drew?"

He motioned for his mother to stand in his place and then led her down a long hallway onto the back balcony. Together they sat on a carved wooden bench near a small garden of potted plants. A pigeon flew onto the cement railing opposite them, flapping its wings and watching with an observant eye.

"How lovely." Jennifer admired the gray wings and turquoise neck.

"I'll have to take David's pots in before winter." Drew rolled his hand over a plant next to him.

"You know what I did the other day?" Jennifer asked and then answered her own question, adding, "I watched your tape."

"We don't even know if Salt Lake will still be held," he said.

"You're going?"

"I couldn't get through that," he added. "You can't give up!"

"If my heart's not in it the judges will know."

"We'll all go," she promised.

Slowly, Drew's eyes filled with tears. "I can't."

"Giving up isn't what David would have wanted." The pigeon on the railing flapped its wings, cooed, and bobbed its head. The patio door burst open, and the bird flew off as Frank joined them.

"There you two are," Frank said. "The Preacher's arrived and wants to say a prayer, Drew." Drew rose to his feet, stuffing his hands in his pockets.

"Would you like to come by tomorrow? I'm having my weekly poker game," Frank offered.

Jennifer gasped, her eyes tightening in rage. "How could you even think of playing poker the day after my brother's funeral?"

"We're just talking."

"Absolutely not," Jennifer said.

Drew interrupted, saying, "I am really bad at cards."

Frank pointed to himself. "A great teacher."

Throwing her hands on her hips, Jennifer angrily reminded them, "My brother is gone! How can you even think of poker at a time like this?"

A delicate woman's voice came from the yard. "Jen."

Jennifer pivoted and discovered Maria in her large hat and high heeled shoes, standing in the back yard. Jennifer was surprised to see her. "Maria?"

"I told Rich I wasn't showing but then changed my mind. Is it okay that I'm here?"

"Of course," Drew replied. "Let's go inside so the preacher can bless the food."

The group traveled among the grieving visitors. Jennifer watched Rich's reaction as Maria came down the hallway. His face brightened the second his eyes met hers.

Maria went to stand next to him and whispered, "With David gone, I realize now that life is too short. I'm going to move out of Jim's so we can start rebuilding our marriage."

Jennifer felt as if she shouldn't be overhearing such a personal conversation. She shied away towards the piano next to Frank, Drew, and the Pastor.

"Let's bow our heads," the Pastor intoned, folding his hands in front of him. "Lord, we ask you to bless this food and those who come to you mourning the loss of David. Be with us and give us strength. Let us remember the wonderful times we've shared with such a great man. Amen."

"Amen," all in attenDrewce replied in unison.

Frank leaned over and whispered in her ear, "You didn't let me finish. Whoever wins the jack pot tomorrow, will donate the money to the September 11th fund. I'm inviting the whole neighborhood. David loved poker, Jennifer. It's his favorite thing. Don't you think he would have wanted to be the 'honorable' winner of my biggest game ever?"

She leaned over, forgivingly. "I'll sit in."

"You?"

"Even me," She watched him plod over to Karl and Charlie and saw the giant smiles wash across their faces. Perhaps Frank was thinking of poker at David's wake, but then again, if it made his friends happy, David would have approved. In fact, he's probably playing in heaven.

CHAPTER 25

Neighbors filled the house surrounding several poker tables in the center of the cleared out living room. Jennifer smiled to Vicky beside her. "Have you been watching the news?"

"The firefighters line up and salute body bags as they carry them to the ambulances."

Shivers rolled down Jennifer's spine. "I heard."

In the center of the players, Frank raised his beer. "Excuse me," his bottle lowered to the center table in front of the larger dealer's chair, "we are all honored by your presence. As you know Jennifer lost her brother and Vicky her fiancé, Larry. These great men will never be forgotten. There were times when both sat across the poker table from us. Today, we come together not just as neighbors, but as one American team." Frank raised two boxes of cards. "On your tables are two sets of cards. One we'll use. The other, please remove a Heart and a King card."

One by one each table's dealer held up two cards.

"Place the Heart in the center of the table. Let this represent Larry Hartman of the police for his heart of courage." Frank lowered the card to the center. "Now take one King and place it beside the heart card. Let this represent David, the King of fires, all the firefighters, our brave kings among men. From now on these cards will stay in the center under each pot. Let none of us ever forget these men were willing to gamble with their lives on September the 11th. They paid the ultimate sacrifice and will forever remain our winners, our heroes."

Everyone began to clap.

"Dealers, begin." Frank sat back down as Charlie started to deal out five cards to Rich, Vicky, Frank, Jennifer and himself. Charlie turned his cards over and so did Jennifer. She had no idea how good her hand was. She had two kings, an ace, and two three of clubs.

Vicky leaned in. "You need help?"

"Yes," Jennifer said.

"Jennifer and I will play together." Vicky scooted down into a chair, then quickly handed Charlie back her cards. Vicky then took all of her money and moved it to the pot.

Frank leaned in from the next table, grinning. "We don't normally play teams, except for today."

Full throttle, the card games began around the room. Jennifer watched as dozens tossed coins into the center while others blurted out requests for new cards. Her home suddenly filled with activity and movement, everyone enjoying themselves.

"I was surprised to see Maria at David's wake," Rich said to her right. "Did you guys invite her here?"

Jennifer asked, "Should I call her?"

"That's okay," Rich said.

Jennifer wondered if she should have. "How heartless of me."

Rich tossed a dollar into the pot. "I'll raise five." He then turned to Jennifer. "That's fine."

Jennifer watched as Frank put in five dollars. "I heard her tell you at the funeral that she wanted to try to work on your relationship. Isn't that what you still want?"

"It would have been best," Rich responded, "if I weren't leaving."

"We need another card." Vicky put their money in and waited for Charlie to hand her one. She flipped it over and showed Jennifer a three of hearts.

"How good is it?"

Vicky whispered in Jennifer's ear, "We have two pairs, but by Rich's smirk he must have a real good hand."

Frank leaned in from another table toward Rich. "You signed up again?"

Charlie didn't toss in his money; he lowered his hand and questioned further, "Back to active duty?"

Rich nodded, his smile growing. "Yes, I'll raise twenty dollars."

"When?" Jennifer questioned as Vicky laid her cards down, folding.

"My plane takes off in the afternoon, but I'm going early to make sure I can get through all the security checks." Rich watched the other players fold at their table.

Vicky said, surprisingly, "But you just got back."

"What about your son?" Jennifer asked.

"Someday he'll understand. I can't sit back and watch my brothers go to war without me."

Jennifer laid her fingers on top of Rich's arm. With tears in her eyes, she said, "Thank you."

Rich revealed his cards, showing a full house, three tens and two five of clubs. Entitled, he won.

CHAPTER 26

At one point Charlie stood up and began telling jokes to the crowd at Jennifer's house. In the background, the television softly broadcast a benefit 9/11 concert. She was pleased joy had come into her house even though sniffles punctuated the chuckles and guffaws.

She gazed over the buffet across the kitchen counter; half the chicken wings and potato chips were gone. All of the Red and Blue kegs of beer were emptied; the white keg was the only one still at the brim.

Rich, the big winner at their table, was grinning again as if he knew this next hand would go his way too. Jennifer had watched enough of Frank's games over the years to recognize Rich's confident expressions. He had even once told her to look for them.

For a moment, her mind drifted back to David. She missed him already. Drew, of course, was near out of his senses too. At least he would try out for Salt Lake. Hopefully it would be a safe experience. Is this what America is coming to? Worrying about safety in our own backyard? she wondered.

"I have to go to the rest room," Vicky said, handing Jennifer her cards. "Stay in the game."

"Are you sure?" Jennifer asked.

Vicky whispered, "No matter what," then she hurried through the tables to the bathroom in the bedroom.

"You still in," Rich asked her, grinning and raising the pot twenty dollars.

Jennifer grimaced. "Yes." She tossed in their money.

"Are you sure?" Rich looked to see that she had two hundred dollars left. "Because I raise you everything you have?" He moved his large pile of cash into the pot.

Jennifer wondered if she should. Vicky and she would be out. She prayed quickly, "David, help me." She reached in and slid the King (of fires) card in front of her chair.

"Watch it. She's got her brother on her side," Charlie warned Rich.

"Let's see what the little lady's got. I've got two pairs, two Queens and two aces." Rich revealed his cards.

"Beats three of a kind," Charlie said.

Jennifer didn't know if she won; she slowly showed her cards, one by one, four Aces and a six. Rich's eyes lit up with surprise. "I won?" Jennifer gasped.

Overhearing, Vicky rushed back to the table. "We did it!"

Frank rose from his table and gave Jennifer a big hug. "Congratulations, your first win."

Jennifer suddenly felt a hand on her shoulder. She turned but no one was there. David?

"Doesn't she look surprised," Frank complimented. Jennifer sat down, catching her breath.

"Well, it looks like the ladies will be in a while longer," Charlie said and laughed.

"Longer than me." Rich pointed at the blank space in front of him. "My money's gone so time for me to call it a night."

Charlie quickly questioned, "Do you know where you'll be stationed? I want to stay in touch."

"First Georgia and then only God knows where." Rich rose. Charlie rose to shake his hand.

Vicky gave Rich a big hug. "We'll miss having you around the neighborhood."

"Keep an eye on Gelsid and my parents for me?" Rich turned to Frank.

"No problem." Frank smiled.

"I've got a lot of packing to do," Rich said as he waved off.

"Have a good night," Charlie said.

"We'll miss you." Jennifer grabbed his hand and tightened her grip. Rich squeezed back, then headed out the door.

Frank announced to the crowd, "Everyone, say 'bye to Rich. Tomorrow, he goes back into the Army!"

Aunt Sophie questioned, shockingly, "What time are you leaving?"

"Three." Rich waved. "You all have a good night." Everyone in the room applauded as he walked out.

CHAPTER 27

After six more hours of continuous poker playing, Charlie proved winner at their table, but Jennifer and Vicky lost most of their money.

Jennifer began to count their chips as well as the pots at several other tables around them. After counting out seven thousand dollars, she checked out the only table still playing, her aunt's. "How's it going?"

"Karl just won our last hand," Aunt Sophie announced, watching him collecting money on their table. "Do you know Karl's collected $7,000 already from all the other tables? This is going to be a huge donation to the 9/11 fund."

"With what I've collected we can double that." Jennifer rolled out her wad to Aunt Sophie. "This is another seven grand!"

"Fourteen thousand dollars!" Aunt Sophie gasped.

Frank took Jennifer's stash. "Actually, the guys voted and decided that half of the winnings should go to you to rebuild your coffee shop." Aunt Sophie's eyes filled with tears as the money was placed in front of her.

"It may be a few months before they clean all that up," Frank said, putting the money in front of her.

Aunt Sophie rose and hugged Frank, Jennifer, and then Karl. "Thank you. I don't know what to say. I know this was all your idea. And, Frank, you don't even like Jennifer working for me."

Frank smiled. "I'm used to it."

"But this is still too much. All I need is three thousand to hold me over until I get the insurance money." Aunt Sophie walked to the phone and dialed a number.

"Hello, is this the September Eleventh Fund?" Aunt Sophie asked. "Yes… well, I'd like to pledge eleven thousand dollars."

"Aunt Sophie, that was for you!" Frank reminded.

She held up a finger to silence him. "Where do we send the check?" Aunt Sophie began to scribble an address on a notepad, gave all her personal information and then hung up.

"That was very kind, even incredible," Jennifer said and gasped.

"I may pledge more." Aunt Sophie grinned. "I'll make sure I have enough for the insurance deductible. The rest will go to the fund."

Jennifer had never been so proud of her aunt before. She rushed over and kissed her cheek. "Everything will be all fine again, right?"

"We'll make it. It's going to be really hard without David, but we'll just have to remember that we are survivors. That's all." Aunt Sophie grabbed her purse and headed out the door. Charlie and Vicky followed her.

Frank kissed Jennifer on the lips. "I don't know about you, but it's four a.m. and I'd really like to get some sleep."

Jennifer locked the front door, then went back to bed. By the time her body laid out, she could hear her snoring husband.

She remembered how much she had hated that when they first got married. His snoring drove her almost to the brink of insanity. After all that had happened, she would have done anything to hear just one more snore. Drifting off into slumber, she rolled over and laid her arm across her husband's expanding chest, enjoying the sound.

* * * *

"Wake up!" Frank touched her shoulder.

Curled up into a ball, Jennifer wiped her eyes and saw the sun shining brightly through the thin white curtains. "What time is it?"

"It's three o'clock in the afternoon. You slept like a baby," Frank announced. "Rich is about to leave. Throw on something."

Jennifer quickly grabbed a dress out of her closet, checking herself in the mirror. She brushed her long hair and rolled on some fuchsia lipstick and hurried to the living room. The front door was opened, and she saw dozens of people lining the street.

She hurried onto the porch. All the neighbors were at the end of their driveways. Many were holding signs reading, "God bless you, Rich," and, "Come home safe."

Frank walked over to her, taking her hand.

Suddenly the garage door opened at Rich's parents' house. The car backed out of the garage, parents sitting in the front. Rich dressed in army uniform had his son right by his side.

Like thunder the neighbors cheered as the car slowly rolled down the street. A hero, Jennifer thought. Rich was a real American hero.

Dozens of children began waving flags. Grandparents started hooting and hollowing praise. Frank pulled Jennifer across the street, following the car, where Vicky suddenly held up her poster reading, "Rich, go kick some ass!"

Rich's eyes filled with tears. He stuck his hand out of the car and began shaking each neighbor's hand, saying, "Thank you," as the car rolled slowly down the street.

"We'll pray for you," Jennifer said back.

"No, thank you!" Frank said.

"Thank you," others added.

"We love you," was repeated.

At the corner stood Maria, covered with tears running down her face. "You come home," she cried out, grabbing at his hand.

The car rolled to a stop. Rich got out and hugged Maria. He kissed her on the lips. She wrapped her arms around him. "Come back! You come back!"

As he re-entered into the car, the crowd waved their flags.

Jennifer watched as Gelsid jumped out, embraced them both, with child- like tears rolling down his pudgy cheeks.

CHAPTER 28

A long black Cadillac pulled into Frank's driveway. Frank turned to Jennifer and said, "Oh no, it's Jack, my boss! Do you think he found out why I was in the Twin Towers?"

The door swung open and out stepped a balding man in a three-piece navy suit. His tie was striped sideways, just like how his hair was combed. His skin was tight but bags appeared under his eyes. The moment he saw Frank across the street among the flag-holders he called, "Frank!"

Taking Jennifer's hand, Frank dashed across the street. Jennifer took one last look at Rich's car as it turned around the bend; she would miss him. He was a good friend and a great man.

"Mr. Peters, how nice of you to come to my home." Jack shook his pudgy hand. "This is my wife, Jennifer."

"Yes, I've heard Frank speak of you before," he said, reaching for Jennifer's hand.

"Would you like to come inside? Can I make you a cup of coffee or maybe some tea or soda, perhaps?"

"Do you have any scotch?" Frank began pondering.

"We have some," Jennifer remembered. "In the upper cabinet with the Captain Morgan rum."

"That's right, come on in." Frank began to escort his superior in.

"That was some sendoff there. Friend of yours?" Jack asked Frank.

"Yes, that's our neighbor's son, Rich. He just went back into active duty for the army."

"I see," Jack Peter's said, unimpressed, choosing to sit in the recliner.

Jennifer hurried for Frank's scotch as he sat opposite Mr. Peters on the sofa. He positioned himself to sit on a rip beneath.

"What can I do for you today, Mr. Peters?" Frank asked.

"Well as you know, we closed the office down since the attack on America."

"Yes, sir."

"President Bush gave a speech last night about how Americans need to get back to work. Did you hear?"

"Yes, sir."

"I think it's best we open on Monday. What do you say?" Jack Peters raised a brow. "We have a lot of work to do on that merger with the phone company."

"I'll be there early Monday."

"Most of the other employees I just gave a call to this morning, Frank, but I wanted to come see you in person."

Jennifer handed Mr. Peters a scotch and gave one to Frank even though she knew he didn't like anything but beer.

"Thanks, Dear."

"No problem." Jennifer sat down beside him, nervously.

"I really appreciate your coming to my home and telling me in person, sir," Frank said.

"Well, I heard some rumors from one of my Paralegals there and she told me that she heard from another Paralegal who works for the Smith office up in the towers and that you had an interview." Jack Peter's leaned back. "I wondered if that had been true. You know how those girls talk."

Frank grimaced without speaking for a moment. "Sir, I'm not one to lie, so I will tell you what happened. I've been waiting for a partnership with your firm for four years now. After Kevin Donley left, I was sure that you would allow me that opportunity. When you took Winters instead, it upset me, temporarily… and I did go for an interview at the firm. Luckily, I made it out alive. My wife's brother didn't. He was a firefighter."

Jack Peters' head suddenly lowered. "I'm sorry, Jennifer, to hear of your loss, so many… these days."

"Yes, thank you." Jennifer gulped.

"So, the rumors were true. Smith was going to offer you the partnership."

"I don't know, sir. I just had my interview and was leaving when the plane hit five stories above."

Jack Peters took a large gulp of scotch. "Smith only hires the best. His firm steals most of our clients."

"I know, sir, but it wasn't an attack on your firm. It's just I feel I'm ready to become a full partner. You've taught me everything I know."

"And you would use that against me?" Jack Peters whispered.

"It didn't seem that way, not until now. But I'm willing to pay my dues. If you feel I'm still not ready, then I'll keep plugging away for you."

"What makes you think I'd want you to stay?" Jack Peters asked. "Now that I know you were willing to stab me in the back after all I've done for you."

"All you've done for him?" Jennifer suddenly got angry. "You haven't given him a raise in… two years."

Frank gave her an angry look, so she immediately stopped.

"So, this is how it is." Jack leaned forward and placed what was left of the scotch on the coffee table. "So, this is what I've made of you, a cutthroat, a lawyer willing to steal my clients?"

"Am I fired?" Frank asked. "Don't beat around the bush, sir. Tell me how it is, and I'll deal with it. If you don't want me there on Monday to work, then I'll clean out my cubicle."

"You will get your stuff out of that cubical immediately," Jack said coldly.

Frank's eyes closed. Jennifer wondered how they would make it without his salary. They could sell her car? The house?

"And move into your own office next to mine?" Jack continued, raising a hand for Frank to shake. "You'll become a full partner on Monday if that's what you still want?"

Frank stood. "Sir?"

"I like you, Frank, always have. I had every intention of making you a full partner. What you didn't know is that Winters wasn't the only man I was going to promote. I was going to tell you the morning you called in sick or more like lied to me about going to the doctors."

Frank shook his hand. "I'm sorry, Sir. It won't happen again."

"Smith only hires the best. And he was right about your potential. I'm pleased you'll be staying on my team."

"Absolutely!" Frank wrapped an arm around Jennifer.

Jack Peters rose and began heading towards the door. "Thanks for the scotch, Jennifer."

"You're welcome, sir."

"See you on Monday, Frank." Jack Peters found his way out.

"Oh my…" Before Jennifer could utter the word, Frank wrapped his arms around her waist, lifted her up and began twirling her around.

"I'm a partner!" he roared. "A partner!"

CHAPTER 29

Jennifer and Frank walked out onto the stoop and watched the neighbors retreat into their houses decorated with flags and signs for Rich. They leaned against one another in an embrace underneath the red, white and blue banner waving on their front porch.

"I can't believe I got promoted," Frank said. "It finally happened!"

"I'm so proud of you! You worked so hard, you deserve it!" Jennifer smiled.

Jennifer sat down on the bench and Frank followed, placing an arm around her shoulders. Slowly, she laid her head on his shoulder. "I'm glad we found something to be happy about, even now."

"Me, too."

"Things are really happening for you now, and it's about time they recognized you as a partner," Jennifer reminded.

"You know when he started talking about going to a competitor's firm, I thought you and I were going to be struggling a while. With the economy and so many people losing their jobs, it would have been a nightmare to find another firm willing to hire me."

"That's true, honey."

"I know that losing your brother was hard and so was Vicky losing Larry. It's just doesn't feel right, you know, why some suffer, and others wind up being okay through it all."

"The whole country suffered," Jennifer concluded. "Don't let that take away from your dreams, Frank. You worked so hard for this. Remember what President Bush said, 'Get back to work. Don't let the terrorists win.'"

"He did say that, didn't he?" Frank shrugged. "And you of all people quoting him; I never thought I'd ever see the day that would happen."

"He did all right through all this, even if Gore did get more overall votes in America."

"You had to just stick that in, didn't you?" Frank laughed, then looked up to the flag. "Do you think I should take it down now?"

"No, I think we should fly it every day for all those who lost their lives."

"Okay." Frank leaned back. "You know this whole thing reminds me of a card game for those in the Twin Towers; it was a gamble who would wind up with the best hand and survive. It could have been anybody who would live and who would die. Somehow I made it out, I wound up alive, and even got a promotion."

"Do you really feel that way about those who made it out of the towers?"

"If everyone were alive, especially David, then maybe I would have felt at least good about getting a better hand."

"I'm happy that you got the promotion, Frank. Let's just concentrate on what we can do to rebuild. We have to find a way to move past all this pain. We have to be strong for ourselves, our neighbors, and all our friends. We'll rebuild Aunt Sophie's Café. We will take more pride in our neighborhood! We're lucky to live here. We are so blessed to live in this country."

Frank kissed her lips and looked up at the flag again. "Yeah, you're right. One nation under God! Let the flag fly."

"Let it fly forever, not just up there, Frank, but in our hearts. We took this country for granted. And I don't know about you, but I can't forgive myself, not now. I should have realized how much America meant to me before September 11th. Taking America for granted ends here and now." Jennifer raised her arms to her neighborhood. "And I am never going to forget that horrific day in September, or any of those who died. I am proud of the people of this country, especially our firefighters, EMTs, police, doctors, nurses and the military; no matter if they are straight or gay, no matter their color, their shape or size, male or female, tall or short, these men and women risk their lives every day for our safety, for our health and to protect our freedom in the greatest country on earth. We are free because of their sacrifices, willingness to help and fearless desire to serve others."

Frank agreed by nodding his head. "You should write a book about our neighborhood. I'm sure it's not much different than the pride in everybody else's."

"Maybe I will." Jennifer smiled. "Maybe I will write about what really makes Americans truly great: that we have heart."

ABOUT THE AUTHOR

Michele Wallace Campanelli is an American writer, singer and celebrity. During the early 1990s, Michele was lead singer of the heavy metal band, Black Widow, which was one of the first all-female bands in Florida during the early 90s. After the band, Michele Wallace Campanelli started writing short stories and fiction novels professionally. She has had nine stories appearing on the best-sellers list, including two that reached #1 on the *New York Times*. Her short stories have been included in over 30 international selling anthologies. She has also penned numerous novels, magazine and newspaper articles in both fiction and non-fiction published by Simon & Schuster, Chronicle Books, Fireside Books, Fictionwise, Florida Today Newspaper, Woman's World Magazine, Adamsmedia, McGraw-Hill, Multnomah Books, Red Rock Press, HCI and America House Publishing. Over 57 million people have read her written works internationally. In 1998, Michele wed Louis V. Campanelli III at St. Mark's UMC in Indialantic, Florida. In June 2012 Louis passed away. She currently lives in Brevard. When Michele isn't writing, she is CEO of Regal Entertainment Services LLC which performs concerts around Florida. She is a professional singer, writer and actor. As a devoted Christian, she uses her talents to glorify God and bring joy to others through music and her books.